Thumbprint Mysteries

DEATH IN THE DESERT

BY

PATRICIA MATTHEWS

CB

CONTEMPORARY BOOKS

a division of NTC/CONTEMPORARY PUBLISHING GROUP
Lincolnwood, Illinois USA

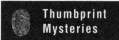

Thumbprint
Mysteries

MORE THUMBPRINT MYSTERIES

by Patricia Matthews:

The Secret of Secco Canyon
Dead Man Riding

This is a work of fiction. The characters, incidents, and dialogues are products of the author's imagination and are not to be construed as real. Any resemblance to actual events or persons, living or dead, is entirely coincidental.

Cover Illustration: Matt Zumbo

ISBN: 0-8092-0608-0

Published by Contemporary Books,
a division of NTC/Contemporary Publishing Group, Inc.,
4255 West Touhy Avenue,
Lincolnwood (Chicago), Illinois 60646-1975 U.S.A.
© 1999 Patricia Matthews
Manufactured in the United States of America.

90 QB 0 9 8 7 6 5 4 3 2 1

PROLOGUE

Juan Gomez had a very bad feeling. For some time
now he had felt a knot of apprehension growing in him.
He had made this same trip a number of times, but never
before had he felt this way.

The back of the van was crowded with Juan and the four
other men with him. It was hot, stifling, in the van. No
outside air reached them, and Hoby Macklin, the coyote,
had told him that the air-conditioning wasn't working.

Part of the bad feeling, Juan knew, sprang from the fact
that he no longer trusted Señor Macklin. For years he had
used Macklin for transport across the border into *El
Norte*, and there had never been any difficulty. The
feeling of distrust had begun during the last trip. Juan
had decided that he would find another coyote soon, but
the time had been too short to change on this trip. . . .

An elbow nudged him in the ribs, and he glanced
around at Pedro. Pedro was one of the four workers Juan

had recruited below the border to work for Señor Owens for the orange picking.

Now Pedro said in a hoarse whisper, "What is wrong, *compadre?* You seem worried, and you're sweating like a pig."

Juan whispered back, "It is too hot in here."

Pedro shrugged. "It is always hot. It is the desert, Juan."

Juan waved him off and lapsed back into his thoughts.

He was worried, very worried, and angry because he did not know the reason for his fear.

He realized that part of the unease he now felt could be because of what had happened last year when he was working in Señor Owens's groves. That incident had been unsettling in itself and had troubled his thoughts during all his time at home this year in Mixtepec.

He jerked his thoughts away from that subject and let his troubled mind be soothed with thoughts of his home and his family. Maria, his wife of fifteen years, and the *niños* were the most important things in his life. It hadn't been until he wed Maria that he had started going north across the border to work every year. Mixtepec was a small village and there was little work to be had. Juan owned a small house and a plot of land upon which he raised a few vegetables and a handful of chickens, but he also needed pesos to buy that which he could not raise.

So after the birth of the first *niño*, Tomas, Juan had started making the yearly trip to *El Norte*. It was a long, wearying journey of fifteen hundred miles from Mixtepec to Sonoyta, just across the border from Lukeville, Arizona. Juan knew he had been fortunate, for that very first year he had found employment with Señor Owens near Phoenix. Every year since, he had worked at least six months in the Owens grove. Most of the money he earned he sent home every month to

Maria. They had been able to use some of the money to make payments on a real farm, so that he would be able to support his family without going to work in the United States every year.

He hoped to finish the payments soon. Perhaps, after what had happened last year, he would make this his last journey north. He had hoped to save a little more, but quitting had been increasingly in his thoughts. He didn't have as much saved as he had originally planned for, but . . .

Abruptly, the van slowed, and Juan was jolted back to the present. The rear windows in the van had been painted over, so the occupants couldn't see out but light could come in, and now the windows were flooded with bright lights coming up from behind.

Why were they slowing? Juan knew that they had passed through the Organ Pipe Cactus National Monument some time ago and were now on the highway leading to Sells. From there they would turn north, pass through the Papago Indian Reservation, and head toward Phoenix. The land they were passing through now was all desert—hot, barren, and unforgiving.

The van came to a jarring stop as an amplified voice bellowed, "Pull over! Now!"

Fear turned Juan's sweat to ice.

At Juan's side Pedro said in a terrified whisper, "*La Migra!*"

Immigration! They all knew that dreaded word. One of the men was already at the door, pushing it open. He piled out, the others on his heels. Juan was dazed but infected by the terror of the others. He followed them out of the van and landed so hard on his feet that he stumbled and fell to his knees.

Quickly, he got to his feet. There was a pickup parked immediately behind the van, its lights blazing. He noticed that the others were scattering like frightened rabbits, fleeing toward the desert on both sides of the road.

Juan started to follow when a voice bellowed, "Juan Gomez!"

Juan froze, squinting into the bright lights. He made out a dim figure standing beside the pickup on the driver's side. There was something vaguely familiar about the voice . . .

Then yellow light bloomed like a deadly flower before the dim figure by the pickup. Something slammed into Juan's chest with sledgehammer force. The sound of a gunshot boomed in the silence of the night, and Juan was slammed back against the back of the van and slid slowly to the ground.

The world dimmed around him and his body felt numb. His last thoughts were: "Maria. *Querida*, forgive me . . ."

CHAPTER 1

As Rob Harding knocked on the office door, a strong voice told him to enter.

When Rob opened the door, the man behind the big desk glanced up, his gray eyes angry. Rob wasn't surprised; Stanley Morgan, supervisor of the Governor's Task Force on Crime, was often angry. Morgan was a short man in his mid-fifties, with blunt features and a snub nose. He was a man of great energy, and even seated he gave the impression of being in motion.

Rob liked Morgan better than any man he had ever worked with. He was intelligent and fair and, most of all, he was fiercely loyal to all of his investigators.

Morgan motioned to the chair before his desk. "Have a seat, Rob." He returned his attention to an open newspaper on his desk.

Rob folded himself into the chair. He was a tall man in his early thirties, well built, with a strong nose and dark gray eyes. His coppery skin showed his Navajo heritage as did his hair, which was black and, though neatly trimmed, was worn long.

Waiting for his supervisor to speak again, Rob glanced around the office. It was surprisingly small and simple for a man of Morgan's authority. The furnishings were plain, serviceable, and inexpensive. One whole wall held several bookcases filled with law books. The only picture in the room sat in a small frame on his desk; it showed Morgan's wife and young daughter, both smiling.

Before accepting the job on the newly formed state task force, Stanley Morgan had been a successful attorney with an important law firm. Rob had always been curious about why Morgan had abandoned his high-paying, well-respected position to take this particular job. The task force had been formed by the governor to investigate crimes difficult for other Arizona law enforcement agencies to handle. There was great need for such a service, but Rob knew that Morgan's job could not be an easy one. Other law enforcement agencies were often touchy about having their turf invaded. As the new kid on the block, the task force was always having to prove itself, and, as its head, Morgan took the brunt of the flak that inevitably came its way.

Morgan finally glanced up. "You read this, Rob?" He turned the newspaper around so that Rob could read the front page.

Rob stared at the article. "I haven't read it, no, but I saw the story on the TV news last night. Terrible thing."

"That it is," Morgan said with an emphatic nod. "Read it."

Rob picked up the paper; the headlines blared: "Four Illegal Workers Found Dead in Desert!"

The story concerned four Latino males found dead

near the Mexican border, not too far from the Papago Indian Reservation. All four had died of exposure in the desert. It was assumed by the Border Patrol that all of the men were workers who had been smuggled across the border from Mexico.

Morgan said, "Now read this."

He handed Rob a page from another newspaper, dated four days ago. Rob looked at the circled article.

"The body of an unidentified man was found this morning on Highway 86, just west of Sells. The man, a Latino, was shot to death and left by the side of the highway. Local law enforcement agencies are investigating."

Rob glanced up at the man across the desk. "You think they are connected?"

Morgan nodded. "It's thought by the Border Patrol that all of the men were part of the same group, even though they were not found in the same location. The man who was shot was found alone; the others were scattered as if they had all been going in different directions."

"Smuggled across the border by a coyote?" Rob asked. Coyotes were men who smuggled illegal workers across the border for exorbitant fees.

Morgan nodded. "They're pretty sure of it, Rob."

"No idea why the one man was shot or why the others were left to die?"

"The usual reasons," Morgan said with a shrug. "Something spooked the coyote, and he didn't want to leave any live witnesses. Or maybe he dumped them just because it was easier than delivering them to their destination. You know how coyotes work; they always get all their money up front."

Rob felt a chill. "That's pretty cold-blooded, sir."

"True, but some of these coyotes have the consciences of snakes. It's happened before."

"Wonder why only one was shot?" Rob speculated. "Why not all of them?"

"The men probably sensed that something was up and scattered like quail," Morgan said. "Hard to shoot five men, all running in different directions, and the coyote probably figured the others would die anyway in the desert. It's brutal country down there, especially in summer."

Rob stared at his supervisor, frowning. "Is the task force going to be involved? It's not exactly our cup of tea; I should think that it's a job for the Border Patrol or the homicide officers in that part of the state."

Morgan looked off. "They're looking into it, of course, but you know how it'll go. If they get lucky and find the killer or killers right away, fine; but if the investigation drags on, their interest will flag. It's human nature, and they have a full plate. Always."

Rob said shrewdly, "That's not all of it, is it, sir?"

Morgan shifted uncomfortably. "Not entirely, no. There's a citrus rancher in the Phoenix area . . . well, the dead illegals were coming to work for him. His address was found on the man that was shot, so we contacted him right away. It seems that the dead man had worked summers and autumns for him for years. You know the drill: they work six months or so, then go back to their families in Mexico until the next season. This rancher feels some responsibility for them. This particular man, he told me, was almost like family. His name was Juan Gomez."

Rob said, "But he's been breaking the law, employing illegals, sir."

Morgan's color rose. "I know, I know, but without illegals, citrus growers couldn't make it. They can't find enough American workers. Americans don't like to do, quote, 'grunt work.'"

"Would this rancher happen to be a friend of yours, sir?" Rob asked.

Morgan glared at him, his mouth set, then sighed and said, "Yes, he's an old friend."

Rob said slowly, "The task force has never gotten involved in a case as a favor for a friend."

"And it isn't this time, Rob!" Morgan snapped. "Well, maybe a little, but I've discussed this with the governor and he's all for us working the case. It's a big problem, Rob. Every year men and women are found dead in the desert. It's giving the state a bad name."

Rob had a tremendous respect for Stanley Morgan, but he didn't like this; it didn't seem right to him. His temper flared, and he said, "So now the buck is being passed to me. Is that it, sir?"

Morgan stiffened, his eyes hot. "Don't you be impertinent with me, young man!" Then he sighed again and scrubbed a hand down over his eyes. "You know me better than that, Rob. The decision is out of my hands; it's already been decided. The task force is to become involved in the investigation. Understand?"

Rob leaned forward. "I think I do, sir, yes. I didn't mean to be insubordinate."

Morgan's glance slid away. "Yes, I know. But watch it."

He passed a hand over his face again, and Rob saw that the older man was gray with fatigue. He gave Rob a tired smile. "You have to understand that in politics, you either compromise or resign. But understand me, Rob. The decision may not have been mine alone, but I agree with it. This situation with illegal workers is a disgrace . . ."

Rob interrupted, "If they could all get green cards,

permission to legally enter the country to work, the situation wouldn't exist, sir."

Morgan's gaze hardened. "That argument has merit, but it is not the law. The task force was created to investigate crimes, and murder is most certainly a crime."

Rob sat back. "Of course. I agree with that. I just don't think it's our job to work this one. Then there's the fact that I'm not exactly an experienced homicide investigator."

"You're my best man, Rob," said Morgan. "I know you've had little experience with homicide, but I happen to think you will do a fine job. You have the intelligence and the instincts for it, and you had a murder during your last case and solved it."

Rob made a negligent gesture. "That was mostly luck."

"You underestimate yourself, Rob," his supervisor said. "You're just the man for this case. Being half Navajo, you can pass for Mexican, and best of all, you speak Spanish like a native. Of course . . ." Morgan narrowed his eyes. "You can always refuse the assignment and it won't be held against you. You know I never assign an investigator to a case against his wishes."

This was true, Rob well knew. Except for one thing: Morgan might say that if Rob refused to take this case it would not be held against him. He might even think that, but Rob well knew that if he refused, it would come back to haunt him some time in the future.

He sighed and said, "Of course I accept it, sir. I sure as hell want to see this killer, or killers, caught and put behind bars."

"Good!" Morgan said heartily. "I was sure you wouldn't let me down. Now . . ." He leaned back. "I know you've had no time to think about it, but how do you think you'll handle the investigation, Rob?"

Rob closed his eyes, thinking hard. After a few minutes he opened them and said slowly, "I suppose the first thing to do is talk to this citrus rancher."

Morgan nodded. "I think that's smart. His name is Thad Owens and his place is located off Highway 89 about halfway between Phoenix and Wickenburg." He gave Rob the exact address and directions on how to find it.

Then Morgan leaned back and contemplated Rob for a few moments before he spoke again. "Just so you'll understand, Rob, Thad and I go back a long way. We went to school together, all through high school. Then we went our separate ways for a few years, but we always kept in close touch. I went to Harvard Law School, and Thad went on to agricultural college.

"Thad has always been interested in politics, but he was never the least bit interested in running for office. He became a power behind the scene, in a manner of speaking. He has quite a bit of clout in Arizona politics and he's a close friend of the present governor, helped get him elected. In fact, Thad was instrumental in getting me this post when I decided I'd had enough of law practice. I told him I was interested in getting into public service— that I wanted to do something really useful—to repay the state for the good life I've had here." He gave a wry smile. "I know that makes me sound like a do-gooder, but it's the way I felt, the way I still feel. Anyway, Thad put in a few good words for me and this job was the result."

"I understand, sir," Rob said.

"Perhaps you do. You're a very perceptive man," Morgan said with a nod. "So you see, I owe Thad Owens, and he's promised to help me get appointed to the bench. It's every attorney's dream, Rob, to become a judge. I wanted you to know and understand all that, but I also want you to understand this." He leaned forward with an intent look. "I don't want that relationship to affect your investigation in any way whatsoever. Is that clear?"

"Very clear, sir," Rob said.

*   *   *

Rob didn't call ahead before visiting Thad Owens. He had learned that it was always best to catch a man he intended to question by surprise. He got better answers that way. This was always a gamble. Owens could be away, but it was a chance Rob felt worth taking.

The drive to the Owens citrus ranch took about an hour. It was mid-July now, and this part of Arizona was like a frying pan. From now until late September or early October, the temperature would reach well over a hundred every day. The sky overhead was cloudless, a blazing, eye-hurting blue. The only respite would come from the monsoon, which, in this area, was just as likely to blow in with stinging dust storms as with rain. If it did bring rain, there was every possibility that it would be in the form of windy gully-washers that would knock down trees and flood the streets.

There was a good chance that Rob would have to be out in the desert near the Mexican border before this investigation was over, and he dreaded the prospect. The heat there would be merciless.

He could smell the ranch long before he reached it: the air became fragrant with the smell of oranges and lemons.

Shortly he turned off onto a well-maintained gravel road. There was no house yet in sight. Both sides of the road were devoted to lines of orange trees, heavy with ripening fruit. The trees were all perfectly aligned, the ground underneath them free of weeds. It was clear to Rob that this was a well-tended grove.

About a half mile down the road, a man suddenly stepped out in front of the pickup. Rob slammed on his brakes, bringing the pickup to a screeching, shuddering stop.

He opened the door and stepped out. The man was coming toward him. He was short, middle-aged, dark. He was wearing sweat-stained work clothes and a floppy straw hat. He looked to be Latino.

In Spanish Rob shouted angrily, "What the devil do you think you're doing, man? You could have been killed!"

The man stopped directly before him, spreading his hands. "I am sorry, señor. I wanted to speak to you. Are you here to inquire about Juan?"

Rob frowned, puzzled. "Juan? Who is Juan?"

"Juan Gomez . . ."

Belatedly, Rob made the connection. Juan Gomez was the name of the man who had been carrying Owens's address, the one who had been shot. "What about Juan Gomez?"

But now the man before him held up a hand for silence and tilted his head as if listening. Then Rob heard the sound of hooves in the grove to his right. Without a word, the man before him turned and glided away, vanishing into the trees. Rob took a step after him, then halted as a big horse galloped out of a row of orange trees and onto the gravel road.

The animal reined in before Rob. The man in the saddle was a big man in his middle fifties. He was bareheaded, a shock of salt-and-pepper hair exposed to the sun. He had a hawk nose and a strong face; his eyes were black as coal. His skin was the color of rich leather from long exposure to the Arizona sun.

He said harshly, "Who are you, mister? I don't recall ever seeing you before."

"My name is Rob Harding," Rob said. "I'm an investigator

for the Governor's Task Force on Crime. My superior, Stanley Morgan, thought I should talk to Mr. Owens. Is that you?"

After a pause, the man seemed to relax a trifle. He tugged at his nose. "Yeah, how is old Stan?"

"Fine, when I saw him a couple of hours ago," Rob said. "Didn't you talk to him just this morning?"

The man's eyes narrowed for just a moment in anger, and Rob thought he was going to explode. Then he relaxed with a burst of hearty laughter. "I did, by God! Just testing you, son, just testing." He kneed the horse closer and stretched his hand down.

Rob shook the extended hand. The man's grip was powerful. Calluses as big as warts lined his palm. *Here is a man*, Rob thought, *who has worked hard and lived hard.*

Rob said, "I'm investigating the deaths of the Latinos in the desert, and I understand one of the men worked for you."

Owens's face tightened. "Ah, yes, poor Juan. Terrible thing. A good worker, worked for me for many years."

Rob thought of the man who stepped in front of the pickup minutes ago, then vanished like a ghost into the grove at the sound of this man's approach. Should he mention that? Caution prevailed. He decided to wait and see what developed. Perhaps it might be better not to mention him at all.

Owens was speaking again. "Come on down to the house. This is no place to talk." He motioned with his head. "The house is a quarter mile down the road."

Without another word Owens wheeled his horse around and urged it into a trot down the road.

Rob got into his pickup and followed.

CHAPTER 2

The Owens house was at least thirty years old, but it had been well taken care of. The earth-toned stucco walls had been painted recently, and flower beds bordered the front of the house. A large lawn, green as pool-table felt, stretched out like a welcoming apron. Weeping willows and tall palm trees gave the place the look of an oasis.

Rob parked in the graveled driveway and waited for Thad Owens to walk up from the stables, which were about fifty yards from the main house.

Rob watched as Owens approached. The older man strode vigorously. His boot heels crunched loudly on the gravel. Without speaking, he motioned for Rob to follow him into the interior of the house, which was dim and cool without the benefit of air-conditioning. The furnishings Rob saw were all dark, heavy, and functional.

Owens led him to the rear of the house and to a room

that stretched the length of the back. It was what was called an Arizona room, walled on three sides by glass. There were several pieces of plain, comfortable furniture, and a number of plants. It was strictly a man's room.

Owens said abruptly, "My wife, Annie, passed on five years ago. Never married again. I've lived here alone ever since she passed. My two boys are hitched and have their own homes in Phoenix." He gave his booming laugh. "Sorry, lad. I'm in the habit of explaining all that to strangers first time in the house."

Owens crossed the room to a well-stocked bar. "I know it's early for the booze route, but I always ride across my acres for a couple of hours every morning. When I get back, I have a jolt to really jump-start my day. Anything for you, lad? Cola? Anything?"

"A cola will be fine."

"Cola it is."

Owens dumped ice cubes into a tall glass, then filled it with cola. He held the glass out, and Rob took it with a muttered, "Thanks."

Owens took down a bottle of Scotch and poured a water glass half full. He tilted his head back and drank it down in one long swallow. He shuddered and set the glass on the bar.

He grinned. "Now I can really start my day."

Now, for the first time, Rob noticed the broken blood vessels on Owens's nose, one sign of a heavy drinker. Owens sat heavily on the couch across from Rob. He crossed his legs. His dusty boots were well worn. He bounced a leg, the pointy-toed boot aimed at Rob like an accusing finger.

Owens said, "So what progress have you made?"

Rob made a startled sound. "I was just given the case a

couple of hours ago, Mr. Owens."

Owens grunted. "Sorry. Didn't mean to sound critical." He grinned slowly. "My late wife always used to say I could make a simple statement like 'I love you' sound like an accusation. So I guess you want to know about Juan?"

"Yes, sir, I do," Rob said. "But first, about the other four. Did you know them as well?"

"Couldn't say until I hear their names. But I doubt it. The way it worked, Juan would spend about six months a year with his family down in Mexico. Then when picking time came around, I'd drop him a note, and he'd recruit the workers we needed for the picking. It varied over the years. Sometime he'd bring a man or two who'd worked for me before. Most often, they'd all be complete strangers to me. What the hell! I may as well be frank here." He gave a shrug. "It's not politically correct these days to admit it, but I never paid that much attention. They all looked pretty much the same to me. It was all done through Juan. He'd pick them out, bring them over, supervise their work, and I'd pay them through him. Worked out just dandy for me over the years."

Rob said, "Paid him in cash, I suppose?"

Owens's eyes turned smoky. "That's right. No taxes withheld, none of that bull. So I'm breaking the law. It's a law I don't believe in." He made a spitting motion. "You going to turn me in, lad?"

Rob said stiffly, "It's not my call. It's not what I'm here for."

"It's what they need, cash," Owens said as if Rob hadn't spoken. "You know what happens most times when illegals are paid by check? They're scared of banks, afraid Immigration will be waiting there to snatch them up. So they go to these check-cashing places who charge them an outrageous fee. Cash is the way I've been doing business for forty years, and I'll continue to do it that way. American workers, even many of the Hispanics with green cards, don't want to dirty their hands picking fruit!"

It was obvious that the man was working himself into a rage. In an effort to divert him, Rob changed the subject. "Juan Gomez. You've known him a long time, then?"

"Ten years, give or take," Owens said with a nod. "The best worker I've ever had."

"He was okay with working here?"

"A happy camper, yeah," Owens replied. "Do you think if he hadn't been, he would have come back year after year?"

"How about the other workers? He get along well with them?" Rob asked.

"Juan got along well with everybody," Owens said. "The thing about Juan, he had dignity, and everybody respected that, liked him for it."

Rob said quickly, "If everybody liked him, why would someone kill him?"

"That's the question, isn't it?" Owens said. "Only one thing I can think of. The coyote who was smuggling Juan over the border figured he was blown for some reason, so he decided to dump his human cargo."

Rob nodded. "That's the obvious answer, of course. But it strikes me as being too obvious, too convenient, and it doesn't answer the question of why Juan was the only one who was shot."

"Sometimes the obvious is just the way it is," Owens said with a quick grin. "Have you heard of Occam's razor?"

Rob shook his head. "I don't think so."

"Well, Occam's razor is the rule that says, more or less, if there are several possible answers to a problem, chances are that the simplest answer is the right one."

Rob smiled. "It sounds like a good rule, in general, but experience has taught me that wherever there are rules, there are a heck of a lot of exceptions."

The older man shrugged. "You could be right, but getting back to coyotes, there's one thing about them that really stinks. They'd kill their own mothers if they felt the need. Something should be done about them. Maybe you're just the one to do it, Harding. At least nail the scum that murdered poor Juan."

"If that was how it happened," Rob muttered.

Owens stared at him keenly. "You have reason to think otherwise, lad?"

Rob thought of the Latino who had stepped into the road in front of his pickup. Should he ask Owens about the man? It seemed pretty certain that he worked on the place.

Instead he said, "How many people are currently employed on your ranch, Mr. Owens?"

"Three, at the moment," Owens replied. "Lola Mendoza, my live-in housekeeper, who's been with me for . . . oh, twelve years, thereabouts. She takes care of the house and cooks my meals." He smiled slightly at Rob's questioning expression. "She's legit, lad. She was born not five miles from here. And there's Jed Hawks. He works for me the year round, seeing that the grove is taken care of. He's legit too. In fact, he's one of yours, if my guess is right. A Papago Indian. You have Indian blood, right?"

Rob nodded. "My mother was Navajo."

"Thought so," Owens said with a nod. "Another man, Carlos. Carlos has a green card and works for me off and on, doing odd jobs around the grove."

Rob wondered if Carlos was the man he'd seen on the road. He said, "Any objection if I talk to them?"

Owens spread his hands. "Nary a one, not if it helps catch a killer. But I think you're wasting your time. The answer lies elsewhere, not with my people."

"Do you know who the coyote was who smuggled Juan across the border? Did he use a particular one or a different one every year?"

Owens shook his head. "No to both qustions."

"But Juan might have confided that information to the people who work here. He might not have wanted to let you in on it, for a number of reasons."

Owens cocked his head to one side, his eyes bright. "You could well be right, Harding. You know something? You're a sharp lad. Always knew Stanley had good judgment. He did right in hiring you." He heaved his bulk to his feet. "Come along and I'll introduce you to Lola."

Rob was surprised when he saw Lola Mendoza. He was expecting a matronly woman in her fifties, but Lola was probably no more than forty, in her prime, with a full figure. Rob felt some embarrassment at his preconceptions. He had typecast the woman before he met her. They found her in the kitchen, baking.

After Owens introduced them, he said, "Lola, the lad wants to ask some questions about Juan. Tell him what you know. I'll be in the Arizona room, Harding. Give me a call when you're done, and I'll introduce you to Hawks and Carlos."

As Owens left the room, Lola gestured to a stool at the center counter. She was rolling pie dough with flour up to her elbows.

She said, "What can I tell you, Mr. Harding? Juan . . ." She made the sign of the cross. "May God be kind to him!"

"What can you tell me about his private life?" Rob asked.

"Very little. Juan's private life was down in Mexico." She raised her head to stare at him, then erupted with a lusty laugh. "Are you hinting that Juan was my lover? No, no, Mr. Harding. It is true that I am a widow, but not Juan."

Rob said hastily, "No, I didn't mean that at all, Lola." Even as he spoke, a stray thought crossed his mind: Could Lola and Owens be having a relationship? If so, what business was it of his? It could have no bearing on Juan's murder.

He said, "What I'm hoping to learn, Lola, concerns the reason for Juan's death. . . . You do know that he was murdered?"

"No, I didn't know!" Lola gasped, a hand going to her mouth. "Mr. Owens just said that he was dead. Why would anyone want to . . . ?"

Rob was nodding. "That is what I'm trying to find out. Do you know of anyone who might have reason to kill Juan?"

Lola shook her head vigorously. "Not Juan. He was a kind, gentle man. I know of no enemies he had."

"He had at least one," Rob said grimly. "He got along well with everyone on the ranch? The men he worked with?"

"No one ever had a harsh word for Juan. He was in charge of the workers he brought up from Mexico to pick the oranges every season. I never heard them speak badly of him."

Rob sighed. This was going nowhere. "How about the coyote who smuggled him over the border every year? It would appear that the coyote, whoever he is, is the most logical suspect at the moment. But I have no idea who he is or why he may have killed Juan. Did Juan ever mention his name to you?"

Lola paused in what she was doing and stared at the ceiling in thought. "No, Mr. Harding, never a name. But he did mention, just last week, that he was going to change from the coyote he had been using."

"Did he give a reason?"

Lola nodded. "He said that the man was cheating those he brought across, charging much more than other coyotes. That was one of the few times I ever heard Juan speak ill of anyone."

"But no names . . . ?" Rob stopped short, belatedly struck by something Lola had said. "You say he told you this just last week? How could he do that? Did he phone you from Mexico?"

Lola looked at him in surprise. "Of course. He always phoned to tell us when to expect him. Mr. Owens wasn't home, so I took the message."

"I wonder why Owens didn't . . ." Rob broke off. "What did he say when he called? Anything you can remember could be helpful."

Lola shrugged. "Just that he was bringing the four other men Mr. Owens needed, and that they were good men. Then he mentioned that this was the last trip he was going to make with this particular coyote."

"How did he seem when he called. Was he upset?"

She shrugged again. "Only when he talked about the coyote; then he sounded angry. I noticed because it was unusual."

"Did he say anything else?"

"No, he . . ." Lola hesitated, then said slowly, "He didn't really say anything else. But now that you mention it, Mr. Harding, he didn't seem quite himself. Usually Juan was real chatty, telling me about his family. He was always after me to come down and visit." Lola laughed quietly.

"This may seem strange to you, but although I'm Chicana, I've never been into Mexico. Somehow I always have the feeling that if I cross the border, I'll never get back into this country again. Silly of me, I know."

Rob waited a moment before getting to his feet. "Thank you, Lola, for your cooperation."

"Did anything I said help?"

Rob said, "I don't know. Maybe."

"Mr. Harding, I hope you catch the person who killed him. Juan was a good man."

Rob nodded. "I'll do my best, Lola, you can be sure."

He went back to the Arizona room. The door was open. Owens stood with his back to Rob, staring out into his backyard. There was a glass in his hand.

Rob knocked lightly on the doorjamb.

Owens turned slowly and came toward him. "Ah, there you are, lad. Did Lola tell you anything helpful?"

"It's too early to tell yet," Rob replied. "But she did raise one question. Why didn't you tell me, Mr. Owens, that Juan phoned here just a few days before his death?"

Owens got a look of surprise. "Why, you didn't ask me. And I didn't think it was important. Is it?"

"It very well could be," Rob said curtly. "Your housekeeper told me that Juan had decided to switch to a different coyote for his next trip. Did you know about that?"

Owens shook his head. "Why, no. Lola gave me his message, but she didn't mention that. I suppose she saw no reason to."

"Tell me, Mr. Owens, did you pay for the coyote?"

Owens said, "Of course. Through Juan. He paid the guy, and then I reimbursed him."

"In cash, I suppose?" Rob said with a touch of sarcasm.

If Owens caught the sarcasm, he ignored it. "I certainly wouldn't pay by check."

"But you don't know the coyote's identity?" Rob asked.

"Not a clue, lad. Juan handled all that."

Rob rubbed his eyes wearily. This was getting him nowhere. "I'd like to talk to your foreman, Jed Hawks, and Carlos now."

Owens nodded. "Of course, lad. Come with me."

They found Jed Hawks in a packing shed on the edge of the grove. He was alone in the shed, inspecting crates. The shed smelled not unpleasantly of oranges.

Hawks was a man in his forties, lean, dark, with a powerful physique. His thick hair was jet-black, and his liquid dark eyes studied Rob curiously as Owens introduced the two men.

After Rob and Hawks shook hands, Owens said, "Rob is with the Governor's Task Force on Crime. He is investigating the death of Juan and the other men down in the desert. He has some questions of you and Carlos." Owens glanced around the shed. "Where is Carlos? Why isn't he helping you?"

"I don't know, Mr. Owens," Hawks said with a shrug of his broad shoulders.

Owens stared. "You don't know?"

"No, sir, I don't," Hawks said. "I've been looking for him for the past half hour. Carlos has disappeared, bag and baggage."

CHAPTER
3

Owens shook his head in disgust. "That's the trouble with too many of these guys; they just decide to walk, and they walk without a word to anybody."

Rob asked, "Was Carlos pretty reliable?"

Hawks looked at him out of hooded eyes. He shrugged, "More reliable than most."

"Then it doesn't strike you as rather strange that he would just walk off like that?"

Hawks said, "A bit strange, yeah, but who knows what gets into people's minds?"

"Has he ever done it before?"

"Nope," Hawks said. "Not since I've been here."

"And how long has that been, Mr. Hawks?"

Hawks thought for a moment. "Be five years next month."

"Was Carlos working here then?" Rob asked.

25

"Nope."

Here's a man with few words, Rob thought. "But Juan was?"

A quick smile moved across Hawks's face. "Juan's been here forever, I think."

"Getting back to Carlos for a moment, did he so much as hint that he was leaving?"

"Not to me."

Owens broke in impatiently, "What's all this with Carlos; what's that got to do with the price of oranges?"

Rob said slowly, "Maybe nothing. Yet it does seem strange that a man who has worked for you for some years would just walk off, particularly since he chose the day I came here investigating Juan's death."

Owens snorted softly. "What's strange? They do it all the time!"

Rob was staring at Hawks. He had detected a hint of animosity in the man's dark eyes. Was it because Hawks had recognized that Rob had Indian blood and thought that he shouldn't be investigating a white man's crime? Yet how would Hawks know, or even suspect, that Juan had been killed by a white man? Or was it because he was harboring guilty knowledge of the crime?

Rob said, "What do you think, Mr. Hawks?"

"How would I know, bro?" Was there a hint of mockery in his voice? "Like Mr. Owens said, it happens all the time."

"About Juan, do you know of any reason someone would kill him?" Rob asked.

Hawks shrugged his broad shoulders. "Nope. You're the detective; it's your job to figure that out."

Rob felt a flare of anger. Hawks was definitely mocking him. He said evenly, "I will. You can be sure of that, Mr. Hawks."

Hawks stared at him steadily for a moment; then some inner tension seemed to drain out of him. He said, "I don't think you'll find anyone around here who would have reason to kill him. Juan had nothing but friends here."

"That's what I keep hearing," Rob said sourly. "Does that apply to Carlos as well?"

"As far as I know," Hawks said. "I never heard any harsh words between them."

"I've found out that Juan was considering changing coyotes," Rob said in an abrupt change of subject. "You have any knowledge of that?"

Hawks shook his head. "Nope, he never mentioned it to me. But then I told him once that I didn't want to know how he traveled back and forth." Hawks glanced sidelong at Owens. "I didn't want to know just in case someone ever questioned me about it."

Rob said, "This other man, Carlos . . . What's his last name?"

Owens looked blank for a moment, then said, "Carlos Ramos."

"Ramos," Rob repeated. "Do you have an address for him?"

Owens looked at the other man. "Jed?"

Hawks shook his head. "He stayed here when he was working in the grove. The rest of the time . . ." He shrugged. "I have no idea. Probably in the area where most of the other Hispanics live."

"But there must have been an address on his identification papers, driver's license, Social Security number, green card?"

Hawks shook his head. "The only I.D. I ever saw was his green card. I didn't check it for an address."

"If you didn't examine it carefully, it could have been counterfeit! You can pick up forged cards almost anywhere."

Owens said, "That's not our concern, lad. Carlos showed a green card. Whether it's faked or not is somebody else's concern."

There was a derisive smile on Hawks's dark face. Rob gnawed his lip in frustration. Was this pair trying to conceal information from him? There was a secretive air about Hawks, but Owens seemed open and aboveboard. Still, he also seemed terribly ignorant about his employees. Of course, Rob knew that wasn't uncommon. Most grove owners hiring aliens tried to distance themselves from them as much as possible.

He said, "Did Carlos perform any grove work for any of your neighbors? Do you even know that much?"

Owens looked at Hawks. "Not to my knowledge. Jed?"

Hawks nodded. "Carlos mentioned doing some grove work from time to time for other grove owners in the neighborhood."

"Which ones?" Rob asked.

Hawks stared at him for a moment in silence before answering. Then he said blandly, "Never mentioned names to me."

Rob looked from one to the other. "That'll be all for now, but I may have some more questions later. Thanks for your cooperation." *Yeah, some cooperation,* he thought angrily; *I could have gotten more information out of a stone.*

He waited until he was back in his truck to use his cell phone. He intended to canvass some of the other grove owners in the area, but first he wanted to talk to his supervisor. Morgan liked to have frequent conversations with his investigators in the field. He wasn't one for written reports.

Rob was put through to Morgan at once. "I just finished interviewing your friend, Thad Owens."

"How did it go with him, Rob?"

"Now all that well, sir," Rob answered. "He talks a whole lot, but he doesn't give out much in the way of information."

Morgan's low laugh came over the line. "Like I said, Thad isn't a politician, but he's been around them all his adult life. He's learned that trick from them; talk a lot but never say anything that can turn and bite you."

Rob said sourly, "That isn't very helpful in an investigation. He's a colorful character, probably even likable under different circumstances, but he's very stingy with facts."

Morgan was silent for a few moments. He finally said, "Is this one of your subtle hints, Rob? You want me to nudge him a little?"

"Well . . . he is your friend, sir."

Morgan laughed softly. "Yes, that's true. I'll call Thad and set up a lunch. Thad likes his booze . . ."

"Yeah, I noticed that," Rob said dryly. "It was well short of noon when I was out at his place, and he had a hefty slug before we talked."

"I'm not surprised, but he can handle it pretty well. He tends to loosen up after a drink or two. I'll wait until he's had a couple, then slip it to him that he needs to talk more freely with you if he hopes to see this killer caught."

Rob said, "Let's hope it works."

"I'll get back to you on that, Rob," Morgan said and hung up the phone.

*   *   *

There weren't too many orange groves left in the area.

Even this far out of Phoenix, developers had moved in like a swarm of locusts. They had bought up the groves, broken them up into small lots, and built houses on the lots.

Rob found three groves that were still intact. The first two grove owners he talked to had never heard of Carlos Ramos, but the third was more helpful. He was a scrawny little man of sixty with big ears and faded blue eyes. His name was Johnson.

To Rob's question he said, "Sure, I know Carlos. He's worked for me off and on for years. Spends most of his time with Thad Owens, but when I need some work done, I call him and he usually comes."

Rob said eagerly, "You have a phone number for Carlos?"

"Sure thing."

"How about his address?" Rob held his breath for the answer.

"Yeah. Let's see if I can remember it." The older man looked heavenward for a few moments, then gave Rob an address in Phoenix. Rob committed the address to memory. He recognized it as being in a barrio.

"Do you happen to know Juan who used to work for Owens?"

The man's gaze sharpened. "Used to? What does that mean?"

"I guess you don't know yet," Rob said. "Juan was shot to death down near the border."

Johnson sucked in his breath. "Terrible. No, I didn't know."

"But did you know Juan, Mr. Johnson?"

"Not well. I spoke to him once or twice when he came by to visit with Carlos."

"They were good friends, Juan and Carlos?" Rob asked.

Johnson nodded. "That was the way I read it."

"The pickers you use . . . Are they illegals?" Rob held up a hand. "Don't worry, Mr. Johnson. I have no interest in immigration problems. I'm investigating a murder here."

"I'm not worried," Johnson said with a snort. "I don't employ illegals. They have to be strictly legit, or I don't use them. Not like Thad Owens and some other grove owners I know." He made a face. "Of course, my grove ain't as large as Thad's, so I don't need as many pickers."

"Then you'd have no dealings with coyotes?"

Johnson said vigorously, "None whatsoever. If I had anything to do with it, all the smugglers would be thrown into jail forever. They victimize the people who come across the border, come over here to work and feed their families."

"Is Carlos truly legit?"

"Oh, yes," Johnson replied. "All the way. He came here ten years ago with his mother and got his green card soon after."

Rob knew that the next question was futile, but he asked it anyway. "All right, you had no dealings with coyotes. But did you ever hear Juan mention the one he used? The way it looks now, the people who smuggled Juan and the workers across killed him."

"Wouldn't surprise me. They're a ruthless bunch. And no, Juan never breathed a word."

"But Carlos might know?"

Johnson nodded. "If anyone would, it'd be Carlos."

*   *   *

The address Johnson had given Rob for Carlos Ramos was located in southwest Phoenix. The area was old and rundown, occupied mostly by Hispanics. Rob knew that youth gangs terrorized the neighborhood.

Most of the houses were shabby and run-down. Here and there one was well tended and neat, a sign that someone still had hope. He drove by one painted a blinding white with a green lawn, recently mowed. This house, located among its shabby neighbors, stood out like a shout.

Rob brought his pickup to a halt before the address he had been given. This house was in poor condition; paint had peeled from the wooden exterior in strips and the unfenced front yard was choked with dying weeds under the blazing summer sun. The screen door in front hung aslant with several holes punched in it.

Rob turned off the motor and sat for a moment, dreading getting out into the blast of mid-afternoon heat. Across the street, two girls of around five or six eyed him curiously. One sat in a swing seat made from an old auto tire hung from a scrubby oak. When they noticed Rob looking at them, they became very busy. One girl began pushing the tire industriously, and the other girl shrieked as the swing took her high.

With a sigh Rob got out of the pickup, bracing himself against the shock of the heat. The weather report had predicted a high of one hundred fifteen degrees today.

The walk leading up to the house was cracked and buckled. There was no doorbell, so Rob knocked and waited. The house seemed as dead and silent as a tomb. He knocked again. Now he heard the slow shuffle of footsteps. The door opened, and a short, dark woman stood in the doorway. She was Hispanic, at least sixty, her black hair streaked with gray threads.

Rob said, "Are you Mrs. Ramos?"

She blinked at him. *"Sí."*

Rob took a card from his pocket and handed it to her.

"My name is Rob Harding. I'm an investigator with the Governor's Task Force on Crime."

Since most of the task force's investigations were conducted undercover, Stanley Morgan had not issued task force identification to his investigators. Rob had ordered cards on his own for use when he wasn't undercover. His supervisor didn't know about it, and Rob knew he'd be unhappy if he ever learned.

Belatedly, Rob realized that the woman was staring at his card without comprehension. Clearly, she didn't read or speak English. He switched to Spanish, explaining what was on the card. Then he asked, "You are the mother of Carlos Ramos, are you not?"

Mrs. Ramos brightened. "*Sí*, señor. Carlos is my son." Then her dark eyes clouded. "Is Carlos in trouble?"

"No, no," Rob hastened to assure her. "I just need to ask him some questions about one of the workers on Mr. Owens's citrus ranch."

The woman wagged her head from side to side. "Carlos is not here. My son is not home."

"Do you expect him soon? He left Mr. Owens's ranch without a word to anyone. I thought he might be needed at home."

Again Mrs. Ramos shook her head in the negative. "Carlos called me this morning. On the telephone. He said he would not be home for some time. He had to go away."

"Go away?" Rob asked. "Go away where, Mrs. Ramos?"

"He did not say, and I did not ask." Her dark eyes shaded with sadness. "My Carlos is a man who goes his own way. He does not ask permission of his mother."

At least he wasn't dead, Rob thought. But why had he fled? He said, "Does the name Juan Gomez mean anything to you? Did your son ever mention the name?"

Mrs. Ramos was already shaking her head. "No, no. Carlos never talks about his work to me."

Rob felt a stab of frustration. He sighed. "All right, Mrs. Ramos. You have my card and phone number. If he calls or comes home, tell him to get in touch with me. Tell him it is the man in the pickup he saw on the Owens ranch. Tell him it's important."

"*Sí*, I will tell him, Señor Harding." Already she was closing the door in his face.

Rob trudged back to his pickup. It was late afternoon, time to call it a day. He had learned very little that could further his investigation, and at the moment he could think of no other avenues to explore. He needed to sit in peace and quiet for a bit and think.

*   *   *

Rob had a small apartment in North Phoenix. Since he spent much of his time out in the field, the apartment wasn't fancy, but it was comfortable enough and often seemed an escape, a haven, from the crime and evil he encountered every day on his job.

It was well after sundown when he parked in his carport and let himself into the apartment. With the sun down, the apartment was dim. He had stopped at a market on the way home and bought a sack of groceries. He carried the groceries over to the kitchen cabinet before turning on a light.

As he set the bag down, some sixth sense warned him that he wasn't alone. He tensed and started to turn. A low voice said, "Don't do anything rash, Harding. Turn slow and easy. I have a gun on you dead center."

CHAPTER 4

Slowly, Rob completed the turn. Jed Hawks stood in the doorway between the kitchen and the living room. A small automatic was nestled in his hand, the muzzle a menacing black hole.

"Well, Mr. Hawks," Rob said in a low voice, "do you intend to shoot me?"

Hawks gave a start and looked down at the gun as if surprised to see it there. He lowered the gun and looked at Rob, grinning faintly. "No, bro, nothing like that. I just wanted to talk. I was afraid that you might pull a gun on me. This . . ." He motioned with the gun. "This was just insurance."

Rob said, "I seldom carry a gun."

"How did I know that? You're a cop, aren't you?"

"In a manner of speaking," Rob said with a shrug. "But my boss doesn't want us to carry except in a possible situation."

"Well, let's hope this isn't a situation." Hawks slipped the gun into his waistband. "Can we go into the living room where we can be comfortable?"

Rob hesitated. "Sure, why not?"

Rob walked past Hawks and into the living room, pausing by the wall to flip a switch. A floor lamp by the couch went on. Rob took a seat on the couch, and Hawks sat in the wing chair opposite him.

"What's a brother doing working for the man?" Hawks asked. "Of course, if I'm right you're not a full blood."

"No, my father was white," Rob said steadily. "My mother was Navajo. As far as that goes, you work for Thad Owens, who's about as Anglo-Saxon as a person can get."

"Different thing. I work, yes, but I don't go around arresting people of my own blood." Hawks's full lips formed a grimace of contempt.

"How do you know I do?" Rob said. "Anyway, as a rule, I don't arrest people. I investigate; other law enforcement people do the arresting when the time comes. But to make my position clear, I believe that anyone who commits a crime should do the time." He gave a hard grin. "You could say that I'm an equal opportunity lawman."

Hawks shrugged. "Whatever you say, bro."

"Look," Rob interrupted, his voice hardening, "why did you come here?"

Hawks locked gazes with him for a long moment, then seemed to relax slightly. "I wanted to talk about Juan Gomez."

"That's funny." Rob leaned forward. "You weren't very informative at the ranch."

"I didn't want to open up in front of Owens."

Rob shook his head. "You didn't have to. You could have gotten me alone easily enough."

"True," Hawks said with a nod, "but I wasn't ready then; I had to think it over for a bit."

Rob's stare was level. "How did you find out where I live? Did you follow me?"

Hawks shook his head. "No, no. It was easy enough. Although your phone isn't listed, I have a friend at the phone company. He ran your address down for me."

"Well, now that you've gone to all that trouble to track me down, what is it you couldn't tell me at the ranch?"

"Not all that much, really." Hawks's shoulders sagged, and he scrubbed a hand down across his face. "I liked Juan. He was a good man, and I'd like to see his killer caught."

"That's what everybody says, but nobody knows anything," Rob said in disgust. "You pass me some hard information, and I might be able to find his killer."

"Something happened," Hawks said. "It was troubling Juan, I know that."

"What happened?" Rob prodded.

"That's the <u>hell</u> of it. I don't know. Juan would never talk about it, but I know that he was troubled. Gradually it seemed to go away until he called me last week. I thought that he seemed . . . well, agitated about something."

"What? Tell me!"

"I don't know!" Hawks said in exasperation. "Juan wouldn't talk about what was troubling him. Juan usually chatted up a storm, but he could be tight-lipped about any personal problems."

"So why did he call you?"

"To check on the number of workers we needed for the picking."

Rob nodded thoughtfully. "Like I said this morning, Lola told me that Juan was upset with his coyote and mentioned to her that he was thinking of changing. Could that be what he was agitated about?"

"I don't think that was it," Hawks said with a shake of his head. "At least not entirely. Juan did tell me that he couldn't change coyotes on such short notice, that he was going to use Macklin this time, but never again."

Rob said alertly, "Macklin? Is that the coyote's name?"

Hawks nodded. "Yeah, Hoby Macklin."

"How come you didn't tell me that you knew about him earlier, at the ranch?"

"Same reason as before. I didn't want to talk before Owens. He's not a bad boss, or I wouldn't have worked there all this time, but he likes to think that he's on top of things. He doesn't like it when he learns that one of his employees knows something he doesn't."

"What else do you know about Hoby Macklin?"

"That's it, his name."

Rob said in a musing voice, "Hoby Macklin. That isn't a Hispanic name."

Hawks shrugged. "You don't have to be a Latino to become a coyote. In fact, most of them aren't. You only have to have a van to start up as a coyote."

"I don't suppose you have an address for him?"

Hawks shook his head. "Nope, but he shouldn't be too hard to find if that's his real name."

"Well, thanks for that much," Rob said.

Hawks looked aggrieved. "I wanted to help all I could, and I want to cooperate all I can, show you that I had nothing to do with any of this."

Rob stared. "You mean Juan's murder? Why would I

think you had anything to do with that?"

Hawks grinned tightly. "You're a cop, right? And a cop thinks in weird ways; like when a Native American is even near the scene of a crime, he's an immediate suspect."

"All right, I'll act like a cop." Rob leaned toward the other man. "Where were you the night that Juan was killed?"

Hawks reared back, startled. "What the hell! I was at the ranch—where else would I be?"

"Anybody who would swear to that?"

"No. I live alone in a small house on the property. Nobody was around that night, not even Carlos. He showed up late for work the next morning. Look, I didn't come here to be questioned about an alibi." Hawks got to his feet, his face darkening.

"What I'm wondering is, why did you come here?" Rob also got to his feet. They stood face-to-face.

Hawks was the first to look away. He muttered, "Not for this, that's for sure. I don't know why I bother to get involved. Now Mr. Owens has left it up to me to call Linda and tell her what happened to Juan."

Rob snapped alert. "Linda? Who's Linda?"

"Linda Gomez," Hawks said. "She's Juan's sister."

"Where is she? Arizona?"

Hawks shook his head. "Nope, down in Mexico. She lives in Juan's hometown. Juan told me she helps out with his family. He can't afford a telephone, so he gave me her number in case I ever had to get in touch with him."

"You haven't called her yet?"

"Nope. I figured I'd try her in the morning," Hawks said.

"Why don't you call her now from here? Save you the cost of a phone call."

"Nope, can't do that." Hawks wagged his head from side to side. "The number's at home so I'll call her in the morning."

Rob said, "You think she'll come up here?"

Hawks shrugged. "How do I know? Could be. They're all big on family, those people."

"Tell her to get in touch with me if she does. I'd like to talk to her."

"I'll tell her, but don't hold your breath, bro." Hawks grinned slyly. "They're not big on cops, those people."

"At least when you find the number, call and give it to me. I will need to talk to her. Maybe I can catch her before she leaves, if she does."

Hawks's glance slid away, and he seemed evasive when he replied, "I'll have to ask her permission to do that, bro. If she says no, I'll have to respect her wishes."

Rob felt a prod of temper. If Hawks had sought him out to help him, why was he being so difficult? Or was he here on a fishing expedition in an attempt to learn how much Rob knew?

He said sourly, "Seems to me you're being pretty noble all of a sudden."

Hawks gave him a flat stare. "Juan was a friend. I owe respect to his sister."

"All right, do what you think best," Rob said with a weary gesture. "Just be sure you call with her phone number."

*   *   *

When Hawks hadn't called by mid-morning of the following day, Rob had a strong feeling that he wasn't going to. He suspected that Hawks had no intention of cooperating further in the investigation. If Rob wanted

Linda Gomez's telephone number, he was going to have to get it himself.

In the beginning, the Governor's Task Force on Crime had had few resources at its disposal, but as time passed and the task force seemed to be succeeding, its budget had grown. Now there was a small research staff available for all its investigators. Rob rarely used the staff, but it was valuable in tracking down people and getting background information on them by computer.

With a grin he recalled his supervisor's derision when the computers were installed in the research department. Morgan had said, "I wonder how investigations were conducted before computers. Whatever happened to good old footwork?" But Rob realized that Morgan was quite aware of just how valuable the computers were to their work.

The research department consisted of three women, all wizards with computers. The only one Rob knew by name was called Mary Sue; he didn't even know her last name. She had a warm, sweet voice, flavored with a touch of the South. He didn't know whether she was married or single, and he hadn't a clue as to her age since he had never seen her.

This morning she answered the phone: "Research Department."

"Mary Sue. Rob Harding."

"Rob! How are you, sweetie?" Her voice warmed noticeably. "I haven't spoken to you in weeks."

Someday, Rob thought, he was going to drop into Research and make the acquaintance of Mary Sue. He said, "I haven't felt the need of your marvelous services."

"Oh! You make me go goose bumps all over!"

Rob had to laugh aloud.

Then, abruptly, she was all business. "What can we do for you, Investigator Harding?"

"I have a name I'd like you to run down. Hoby Macklin. Address, phone number, past history. All I know is that he's supposed to be a coyote working the border."

"One of those!" Mary Sue managed to make a spitting sound over the phone. "Scum of the earth."

"No argument there." Rob had a thought—maybe he could bypass Hawks. "Mary Sue, can you dig up a phone number in Mexico for me? I have only a name and the city, nothing else."

He heard Mary Sue's warm laugh. "We can give it a shot, sweetie. We try hard, but Mexican telephone service being what it is, sometimes it takes a miracle. Miracles, you know, take us a little longer. Give me the name."

Rob said, "Linda Gomez. In San Juan Mixtepec."

"Got you," Mary Sue said crisply. "I'll get back to you. Keep close to your cell phone."

She hung up before Rob could respond. He knew that if it were possible, Mary Sue would come through for him. Finding Hoby Macklin was probably his best lead at the moment. Also, a conversation with Linda Gomez might be helpful.

Rob decided that he would not go out just yet. If Mary Sue could find Macklin's address, it would save him a lot of running around. If not, he would embark on the hunt for Macklin on his own.

Stanley Morgan wasn't hot on written reports. He much preferred his investigators to report to him in person. He had once told Rob: "It's much easier to lie on paper, but I defy any man to lie to me face-to-face." It had been on the tip of Rob's tongue to ask why an investigator would lie to his supervisor, orally or by writing, but a nudge of caution had warned him to keep his mouth shut.

Written reports or not, on his last two cases Rob had gotten into the habit of making notes to himself. He would make a sort of rough outline of the pertinent facts of his case. A retired homicide man from the Phoenix police had told him: "You'll find it helps, Harding, to put facts down on paper. For one thing, it helps insure that you won't forget these facts, and it will surprise you how much it stimulates the thought processes to transfer your thoughts to paper. Try it, you might like it!"

Rob had found this advice to be true. He sat down now at the kitchen table in his small kitchen with a yellow pad and a pen. At the top of the page he wrote in capital letters: "THOUGHTS ON THE JUAN GOMEZ CASE."

Then he paused as a thought struck him. This was the first time he wasn't working a case undercover! He didn't know exactly how he felt about it. There was one thing that he did like. On all his undercover cases Rob had been forced to take on an assumed name, a whole new identity, and he didn't much care for it. As he had told Morgan once: "Sometimes, when I wake up in the morning, I don't know who I really am." It was a relief to be working as himself.

He stared at the blank page. When it came right down to it, he had so far collected little information. There were certainly no hard facts. He made a list of the people he had talked to and people he needed to talk to.

Rob had learned early that three things were needed to solve any crime: motive, means, and opportunity. He wrote the three words as separate headings.

Motive? He had to leave that blank for the time being. The four strongest motives for murder were money, love, revenge, and fear. He didn't see how money could be involved in the murder of Juan Gomez. How could a Latino grove worker be involved in something with a sum of money large enough to motivate his murder? Love didn't seem logical, either. From all accounts Juan had been a happy family man. Revenge? According to all Rob had been told, Juan had been a kind, gentle man, hardly someone to arouse feelings of revenge. The same logic applied to fear. Who could have feared Juan enough to kill him? Of course, there were other, less obvious motives for murder, but at the moment Rob couldn't think of any.

He looked at the other two headings. He failed to see how any of the people to whom he had talked so far could have had the opportunity to kill Juan over a hundred miles to the south. And the means employed had been a gun, which hadn't been found at the scene of the crime. It could have been discarded in the desert, and it might never be found.

He looked at all the empty space underneath the three headings and sighed. He had zilch. Of course it was early yet and . . .

Rob's cell phone rang. With a sense of relief, he flipped it open. Anything to break the monotony of the so-called fact sheets he was trying to work up.

It was Mary Sue from Research. "No miracle has yet occurred, sweetie."

"Bad news, you mean?"

"Depends on how you look at it, I guess. About Hoby Macklin, no address, no phone number. In fact, he seems to have disappeared, but he does have a sheet. An assault-and-battery charge dropped because complainant backed off. Twice arrested for smuggling illegals across the border. Neither charge stuck."

"That sounds like the man I'm looking for," Rob said. "But you've had no luck locating him?"

"Afraid not, but I'll keep looking. I did pick up one tidbit that might help. The last time he was arrested as a coyote, he had a buddy along who was also charged and released. Man named Steve Brack. Him, I have a recent address for."

She gave him an address in Chandler, and Rob jotted it down.

"Now, Linda Gomez," Mary Sue went on. "She exists, all right, at an address in Mixtepec, but no luck with a phone number. I chatted up an operator down there, got right friendly with her. She swore to me that Linda Gomez does not have a telephone number."

"Then Hawks lied to me," Rob muttered.

"Beg pardon, sweetie?"

"Not important, Mary Sue. Just some knuckles I'm going to have to rap. That's all you found out?"

"That's it, Rob. Sorry. I will keep after this Macklin; maybe the miracle will occur."

"Thanks, Mary Sue. I appreciate your help."

After he disconnected, Rob sat for a few moments, staring blindly at the wall. Why had Jed Hawks lied about having a telephone number for Linda Gomez?

CHAPTER 5

Getting a rein on his mounting temper, Rob looked up the phone number for Jed Hawks. But why should he let himself grow angry? He should be accustomed to people lying to him by now. He had noted this phenomenon before: many people seemed compelled to lie to an investigator, even if they were innocent of any crime.

Another old-time cop had once told him: "Lying is an occupational hazard in the cop business, kid. Expect it and you won't be disappointed."

The phone rang several times before it was picked up on the other end and a breathless voice said, "Hello?"

Rob recognized the voice; it was that of Lola, Owens's housekeeper.

He said, "Lola? This is Rob Harding. . . ."

"I remember you, Mr. Harding," she said with a smile in her voice. "But Mr. Owens isn't here. He won't be back until late."

"No, it isn't Owens I want to talk to," Rob said. "Jed Hawks gave me this number to call. Can I speak to him?"

There was a moment's hesitation on the other end of the line, then Lola said, "I haven't seen Jed this morning, Mr. Harding. I don't think he's here. Can I take a message?"

Now it was Rob's turn to hesitate. It looked very much as if Hawks were avoiding him. He sighed. "You might mention to him that I am going to talk to him sooner or later, so he might as well make it sooner or face a charge of obstruction of justice. Got that?"

"Yes, and I'll be sure he gets the message. He could stand being taken down a peg or two."

After hanging up, Rob got a cold drink from the refrigerator and sat down at the table. Instead of returning to his charts, he sat sipping the cola and gazing back into the past.

He had run into this sort of thing before . . .

Rob's father had been Paul Harding, a big, bluff man who had been given to brawling while growing up in Holbrook, Arizona, near the Navajo and Hopi Reservations. Rob's mother, Shona, had been raised on the Navajo Reservation and had attended high school in Holbrook. Other Hopi and Navajo youths attended school in Holbrook, and Rob would probably have been accepted as one of them except for two things—he was only half Navajo, and Paul Harding was a cop in Holbrook. Early on, Rob learned that a half-breed was scorned by some people on both sides. Also, Native Americans were not kindly inclined toward law enforcement officers in general, particularly white law enforcement officers.

So Rob was doubly scorned and was forced into the role of outsider. By the time he was in high school, he walked alone. This didn't bother him too much; he had slowly come to realize that he was pretty much of a loner anyway. But, unfortunately, he was not allowed to just go his own way. He was subjected to taunts and sometimes physical abuse. He was large enough physically to hold his own in the frequent fights, and eventually the other boys walked warily around him.

But the verbal abuse hurt, no matter how much he tried to tell himself it didn't matter. By the time he was ready to graduate from high school, he understood that, generally speaking, Native Americans detested one of their own being associated with the police in any way. It didn't matter that it was his father, not Rob himself, who was the cop. He was hated too. Later, he came to realize that this attitude was what drove him to leave home and join the Army immediately after getting his high school diploma, and it probably contributed to his joining the task force after the Army.

Rob shook his head sharply, clearing his head of thoughts of the past, of slights and prejudices. He should have hardened to it by this time and should be adult enough to ignore all such insults.

He looked down at the page of paper, blank except for the headings. It was time he got out into the field and dug up some facts to fill up the pages. He had lost over half a day waiting for somebody else to help him do his job.

He left the air-conditioned apartment, bracing himself for the blast of heat. In his truck, he started the motor and punched on the air conditioner, leaving the door open for a few minutes to let all the hot air trapped inside the cab to escape.

From the glove compartment he dug out an atlas of

Phoenix and looked up the address Mary Sue had given him for Steve Brack.

*   *   *

The neighborhood in Chandler where the Brack residence was located was several steps up from the area where Carlos Ramos's mother lived. It certainly couldn't be considered a barrio, and the Brack house was neat and well taken care of.

Rob thumbed the doorbell, and it was answered almost immediately by a small woman in her forties, who stared at him with brown eyes filled with apprehension.

"Mrs. Brack?"

The woman gave a birdlike nod. "Yes, I'm Billie Brack," she said in a slightly breathless voice.

Rob asked, "I'd like to speak with your husband. Is he in?"

Mrs. Brack drew in a deep breath. "Are you with the police? Is Steve in trouble?"

"No, no," Rob said with a shake of his head. "Nothing like that. I'd just like to ask him a few questions. I'm not with the police. I work for a state task force." He feared that if he mentioned the word *murder*, she would slam the door in his face and hide in the dark like a rabbit diving into its burrow. "Your husband isn't in any trouble, I assure you."

Her shoulders slumped in relief. "Steve clerks in a hardware store. It's a good job, and he's worked there for two years." She gave him directions on how to find the hardware store.

Rob thanked her and left. Probably she would call her husband and warn him that someone was looking for him, but there was no help for that now. This was always a risk in such a situation. He could only hope that Steve Brack didn't panic and run.

The hardware store was only ten minutes away. It was a large store, located in a mini-mall. The store wasn't too crowded, for which Rob was grateful. The woman at the cash register directed him to the back where he found a slight, slender man, wearing a gray smock, stocking shelves.

Rob walked up to him. "Steven Brack?"

The man turned quickly, almost dropping the items in his hands. *Yeah*, Rob thought wryly, *she called and warned him*.

The man had a narrow face with deep-set gray eyes shadowed with fear. "Yes, I'm Steve Brack. My wife called . . ." He stopped, coughed to clear his throat, and said in a rush, "I've been clean for two years, I swear!"

"Relax, Mr. Brack," Rob said easily. "You're not in any trouble. Do you have a break coming up?"

Brack looked both ways along the aisle. "I usually get a coffee break about this time."

"I saw a coffee shop a few doors over," Rob said. "How about having coffee with me, or a cold drink?"

Brack nodded, whipped off his smock, and hung it on a hook. They walked toward the front. Brack paused by the cash register. "I'm taking my break now, Lucy."

Lucy, busy checking out a customer, nodded without looking up. Outside the store, Rob and Brack turned toward the coffee shop.

Rob said, "My name's Rob Harding. I'm with the Governor's Task Force on Crime . . ."

"Oh, my God!" Brack skidded to a stop, his face alive with panic.

"Don't worry yourself, Mr. Brack," Rob said with a wave of his hand. "You're in no trouble. You have my word."

Brack subsided, but he still eyed Rob askance when

they were in a booth in the coffee shop. Rob waited until their colas were served before speaking.

"Did you hear about the deaths of the illegals down in the desert, Mr. Brack?"

Brack tensed, his hands on the table making pushing motions. "I heard about it on the TV, but I had nothing to do with it. I swear!"

"Relax, Mr. Brack. I didn't say you did," Rob said with what he hoped was a reassuring smile. "You know Hoby Macklin, don't you? You once worked with him, right?"

"So that's what this is about!" Brack seemed to relax a little. "Yes, I know Hoby. And I once worked with him. At the time I couldn't get a job. I was desperate. Billie— that's my wife—she was sick and we needed money for hospital bills, but that was two years ago. I haven't worked with Hoby since. I swear it's the truth!"

"I believe you, Mr. Brack," Rob said soothingly. "Tell me what you know about Hoby Macklin. For instance, how long have you known him?"

"We went to high school together," Brack said. "After high school we sort of drifted apart. I worked at this job and that job. I'd run into Hoby every now and again, maybe have a drink or two with him in a bar.

"Then, four years ago, I met Billie and we got married. At the time I was working at Sears in sales. I got fired. They said I was stealing. I swear it wasn't true!"

Rob held up a calming hand. "I believe you, Mr. Brack."

Brack rushed on, "But the word got around. I stopped giving Sears as a reference when I applied for a job, but it didn't seem to matter. They knew anyway. I ran into Hoby and told him how hard up I was. He told me what he was doing, how he was pulling in the bucks . . ."

"Smuggling illegal workers across the border."

Brack nodded reluctantly. "Yeah, that was it. He made it sound pretty innocent. Said it didn't harm anybody, that it was only against the law because American workers didn't want to do stoop labor but didn't want the Latinos from Mexico to do that work, either. Well . . ." Brack drew a deep breath. "Hoby said he could use me, for good money. I took him up on his offer. I really needed the money, Mr. Harding!"

"How long did you work for him?" Rob asked.

Brack thought for a moment. "About six months. I figure we made about twenty trips altogether. But I was always on the lookout for a job. Illegal smuggling made me nervous as hell, Mr. Harding. I got out as soon as I could."

"Did Macklin always use the area around Organ Pipe National Park to smuggle the illegals in?"

Brack nodded. "Every trip I made with him. He said the best routes were in that area, and all the tourist trade helped because it caused heavy vehicle traffic. Also, he said, it was a good place to dump the Latinos in case he had to."

Rob leaned across the table alertly. "Did he ever do that while you worked with him?"

Brack wagged his head from side to side. "Never. Not once. Everything went smooth as silk. Hoby is good."

"Well, apparently he isn't all that good. He certainly got into trouble with this last bunch. He's a murder suspect now."

"I find it hard to believe that Hoby killed anyone," Brack said with a frown. "Oh, he's wild, with little respect for the law, but kill anyone? No way!"

"I've found that almost all people will kill if they have a strong enough motive," Rob said. "The illegal who was shot was named Juan Gomez. Was he ever in any of the groups smuggled across when you were with Macklin?"

Brack took some time to think again. Finally he shook his head slowly. "Nope, not that I can recall. Of course, you have to understand that I was seldom introduced to any of our passengers." He gave a short, nervous laugh.

"Okay, now to the big question," Rob said. "Do you know where Hoby Macklin is?"

Brack shook his head vigorously. "Not a clue. And I haven't seen or heard from him since I left him. I think he was a little ticked off about that."

"You have no current address or phone number?"

"No, I don't. In fact, I never did. Not for years. When I was working with Hoby, he would always call me. Never gave me a phone number."

Rob studied him intently. He appeared to be telling the truth. Rob had always considered himself very good at telling if he were being lied to or not, but there had been a few times when he had been wrong.

He said, "Didn't that strike you as a little strange, that you were working with a man and had no address or phone number for him?"

"No question," Brack said without hesitation. "But then Hoby is a little weird, like I just said. Always has been. I asked him once why he was so secretive, and he said it was better that way. If the cops came sniffing around, I couldn't tell them how to find him."

Rob said, "Like now?"

Brack smiled slightly. "Yep, like now."

Rob leaned back with a sigh. He drained the last of his cold drink in a gulp, his gaze never leaving the man across the table.

Brack shifted uneasily and glanced at his wristwatch. "Look, I have to be getting back."

Rob nodded. "In a minute. Describe Macklin for me."

"He's about forty-five, my age. He's tall, about six feet. He has dark hair and eyes, and his skin is pretty dark too. His hair's getting thin; he has a bald spot on top. He's not particularly good-looking—a broken nose from high-school football. He keeps himself in pretty good shape. He told me once that he runs five miles a day when he's home."

Brack grinned briefly. "Told me that he might need to run fast one day to get away from the Border Patrol. Oh, and a small scar on his right cheek. Got in a fight once and the other guy wore a ring. I guess that's about it."

Rob said admiringly, "Couldn't ask for more. I wish all witnesses were as observant."

Brack smiled again. "I've always had a good eye for detail. Can I go now?"

Rob nodded. "Just one more thing. What kind of car does Macklin use to ferry the illegals?"

"A van," Brack said promptly. "A black van."

"Thanks," Rob said. "I appreciate your being straight with me. You can go back to work now."

Brack started to slide out of the booth, then stopped. "Is any of this going to get out? You know I was busted once with Hoby for smuggling illegals, but we were never charged. My boss at the store doesn't know that . . ."

Rob interrupted with a shake of his head. "If you've spoken the truth here and weren't involved more than you've told me, none of what you told me will get out."

"It's the truth, I swear!" Brack said fervently.

"Good." Rob waved a hand. "Go to work, Mr. Brack."

Rob watched Brack hurry out of the cafe. Then he placed money on the table for the drinks and a tip and walked out. As he started the pickup and sat in the cab for a few moments to let the hot air escape, he mulled over what he had learned from Brack.

He had learned very little except that now he had a description of Macklin. Rob was puzzled as to Macklin's disappearance. Why had he dropped out of sight? Could he have been killed and his body disposed of?

And there was Carlos's disappearance. At least Carlos had still been alive yesterday, but why had both men made themselves scarce?

Rob sighed and drove off the lot. It was late in the afternoon now, and he didn't look forward to sitting at home alone for the evening.

At a newspaper box at a convenience store he picked up a paper and leafed through the entertainment section. There were a couple of movies that seemed interesting, and both theaters were located not far away.

The one he picked was a mystery movie. While on a case not too long ago, he had watched an old movie on late-night TV and something in the film had triggered an idea that had directly led him toward a solution of the case. Maybe it would happen again.

Two hours later he exited the movie, entertained but not enlightened. The cop in the movie had wise-cracked his way through the two-hour film, crashed a car, shot a suspect, and then came up with the killer out of thin air. At least so far as Rob could see. Too bad it wasn't that easy in real life.

As far as giving him ideas, the movie had been a waste of time. On the way home he stopped at a Mexican restaurant and had a leisurely dinner. It was close to ten o'clock when he left the restaurant and started the half-hour ride to his apartment.

The street on which Rob lived usually had very little traffic. The area was a new development, and there were many vacant lots not built on as yet.

Two blocks away from his apartment building, Rob saw headlights in his rearview mirror. A vehicle was moving up fast behind him, too fast for a residential neighborhood. Then the car was right on his bumper. Now it moved out to pass. The street was quite narrow. Rob pulled over as far as he could on his right.

"Another idiot driver!" Rob muttered.

As the other car drew abreast of him, Rob glanced over. The vehicle was a van, black in color. Then Rob noticed that the passenger-side window was down.

The two vehicles passed under a streetlight. The light, splashing into the other car, revealed the other driver for a moment and reflected from the surface of something metallic.

Rob went tense. The driver was pointing a gun at him!

Even as the thought crossed Rob's mind, he saw a muzzle flash. His window shattered, showering Rob with glass. The bullet whistled past him bare inches from his nose and then passed on, shattering the other window.

Rob risked another glance at the van. The vehicle was still even with him, and the driver still had the gun aimed at him. Rob knew that he was about to fire again, and the odds were that he wouldn't miss a second time.

Chapter 6

Rob lifted his foot from the accelerator and slammed his foot on the brake pedal; there wasn't time for anything else. The brakes grabbed and the tires screamed shrilly as the wheels locked.

Out of the corner of his eye, he glimpsed an orange flare as the driver of the van fired again. This time Rob's pickup had already dropped back enough for the bullet to miss the cab completely.

The pickup was yawing from side to side wildly. Rob took his foot off the brake and fought to get the vehicle under control. The black van shot ahead. Rob risked a single glance at the license plate; predictably, it was smeared with mud and unreadable.

As Rob brought the pickup to a stop, brake lights flashed red as the van hesitated. Then the driver accelerated and raced ahead. At the end of the block the vehicle turned right and disappeared from Rob's view.

Rob sat for a few moments, shaken and stunned by the sudden attack. He thought briefly of giving chase, then gave it up. It would be a waste of time; the van was long gone.

A thought popped into his head. Did the van belong to Hoby Macklin? There was little doubt that the van driver's intent had been to kill him, and there could be only one reason for that. Was he getting close enough to the truth to make Juan's killer nervous?

He laughed shakily. *If I am*, Rob thought, *you could've fooled me!*

Taking a deep breath, he picked up his cellular phone. In the beginning Stanley Morgan had given clear instructions—anytime there was a problem, he was always available to his investigators, day or night.

Rob punched out his supervisor's home number. The receiver on the other end was picked up on the third ring. "Hello?"

"Mr. Morgan, Rob Harding."

"Yes, Rob? What's the problem?"

"I'm in my pickup on my way home. Someone just . . ." For a moment his voice failed him, as the full knowledge of just how close he had come to death crashed in on him.

"Yes, Rob, what is it?" Morgan asked, concern evident in his voice.

"Someone just tried to kill me," Rob said. "A guy in a van drove up alongside me and fired two shots at me."

"Were you hit, Rob?"

Rob laughed without humor. "Didn't touch me, but he didn't do my pickup any good. Blew out both side windows."

"The budget will stand good for it. Thank God you're okay." Morgan paused for a moment. "I don't suppose you got a license plate or anything else to identify the van?"

"No, sir. The license was smeared with mud, and the van was black. Wait . . . There was one thing: the back window was painted black."

"Not much there then," Morgan said thoughtfully. "Tell me which direction your investigation is running. Maybe we can point a finger at somebody who's getting worried."

Quickly, Rob related everything that had happened during the day.

When Rob was finished, Morgan said, "Isn't much, is it?"

"No, sir, it isn't. The only thing I can think of is that the coyote, Hoby Macklin, has somehow learned that I'm looking for him, and he doesn't want to be found. I've learned that Macklin drives a black van. I know it's thin, but that's all I have at the moment."

"Yes, Macklin would be the logical suspect," the supervisor said slowly. "Have you called the Phoenix police about the shooting?"

"Not yet. I thought I'd run it past you first."

There was a silence on the other end of the line. Finally Morgan said, "I don't see what we have to gain. You have nothing that would give them a lead to tracking down the vehicle, and the first thing they would ask you is, do you know of anyone who would want to kill you? You would have to lie. If you told the truth, that would open up a whole can of worms. I always like to cooperate with the local police, but in this case, no. Just keep quiet about it."

"That was my thinking, sir."

Morgan asked, "So what is your next move, Rob?"

"Well, Hoby Macklin is our strongest suspect, but he doesn't seem to be anchored anywhere; it's going to be difficult to find him. Mary Sue, in the research department, is looking for him via computer. Hopefully, she'll find some thread leading to his whereabouts. Meanwhile, I need to talk to Jed Hawks again. Have you managed to speak to Mr. Owens yet?"

"Oh, glad you reminded me, Rob," Morgan said. "I'm taking Thad to dinner Wednesday night. It's the earliest I could manage. Give me a buzz at home about ten Wednesday night, and I'll fill you in."

"Okay," Rob said. He hesitated. "I'm going to have to talk to the guy from the Border Patrol whose case this is. Perhaps you could ease the way for me. He'll probably cooperate better with a call from you."

"Yes. Let's see . . . Yes, his name is Clint Barker. I'll call him first thing in the morning. I'll buzz you when I've talked with him." The supervisor paused. "Rob, I know I don't have to tell you this, but be careful, okay? You're a target for someone out there, so keep your guard up."

"I will, sir. You can depend on that."

After Rob punched off the cell phone, he sat slumped on the seat for some time. Now that the spurt of adrenaline caused by the encounter had subsided, he was drained and exhausted.

Had the driver of the van really been Hoby Macklin? He was certainly the most logical suspect. The question of how he had found Rob was unanswerable at this time. It could have been done any number of ways. One was that Hawks had told him, but why would Hawks have done that? Another question for which Rob had no answer.

What if Hawks himself had been the driver of the van?

Rob cast his thoughts back to those few seconds when he had caught a glimpse of the driver. He'd never had a clear look at the man. The gun aimed at him and the shots had commanded all of his attention.

He shook his head; it was hopeless. He had simply never gotten a good look at the driver. He hadn't the least idea what he looked like. The fact that Rob happened to dislike Jed Hawks wasn't reason enough to suspect him of every crime in the book.

Rob started the pickup and drove on home.

*   *   *

The first thing he did the next morning was take the pickup to a nearby body shop that he had used before. He couldn't drive the pickup around in the Arizona heat without windows. He was lucky that the shop wasn't too busy, and the owner promised that he would have new windows installed by the end of the day. In addition, he had a vehicle on hand that he let Rob have for the day— for a fee, of course.

The loan car was three years old, a four-door, and it was balky and difficult to drive. Rob found himself cursing several times before he reached the Owens Ranch.

He drove past the main house to the area behind the packing shed, where there was a bunkhouse of sorts. It was empty at the moment. A few yards removed from the bunkhouse was a small house. Rob knocked on the door several times. There was no response.

Finally, he walked over to the packing shed. It was empty, the floor ringing hollowly under the sound of his footsteps. He walked on through it and up to the main house. He could only hope that Lola was there.

He rang the bell several times and was about to give up when he heard the sound of footsteps. The door was flung open, and an obviously annoyed Lola glared out at him.

"There is no one at home . . ." She broke off as she recognized Rob. "Oh! Mr. Harding, I'm sorry. I thought it was some salesman. Mr. Owens is out of town, won't be back for another two days."

"Yes, I know," Rob said. "But I'm looking for Jed Hawks."

"That one!" Lola made a spitting noise. "He hasn't been around while Mr. Owens is gone. He often does that, sneaks off somewhere when the boss is away."

"You have any idea where he goes?"

Lola shrugged shapely shoulders. "Who knows? I don't." She thought for a few moments, her eyes closed. "I'm trying to think. He has a girlfriend. He told me her name once . . . Janice . . . that's it, Janice Rust! Jed told me I could call there but only in an emergency. Is this an emergency, Mr. Harding?" Her look was arch.

Rob said grimly, "It's an emergency if you consider catching Juan's killer an emergency."

She got a startled look. "You mean, you think Jed . . . ?"

Rob interrupted. "No, no, nothing like that. I need some questions answered. For some reason, he lied to me."

Lola grimaced. "Sometimes I think Jed would rather lie than tell the truth. Wait, Mr. Harding, I'll get the girlfriend's address."

When Lola returned with the address written down on a piece of paper, Rob asked, "I think I've learned the name of the coyote Juan used, Hoby Macklin. Name mean anything to you, Lola?"

Lola was silent for a moment in thought. Then she shook her head. "No, I'm sorry, Mr. Harding. It doesn't mean a thing."

*　　*　　*

Thirty minutes later Rob parked the loaner in a lot before an apartment house about five miles from the Owens grove. The apartment number Lola had given him was on the second floor. The building was at least twenty years old, but it was in good repair.

He rapped his knuckles on the door. His knock was answered by the thump of heavy footsteps, and the door opened a few inches. Hawks squinted at him. As recognition dawned, the door started to slam shut.

Rob jammed his foot in the narrowing crack. He said, "I want a few words with you, Hawks."

Hawks scowled. "I've told you all I know, Harding!"

"I don't think so. But I do know you lied to me."

Hawks threw his weight against the door, but Rob's booted foot served as a doorstop. Rob said, "If you don't let me in, I'm going to think you're avoiding me and I'll come back with a warrant. I don't think you want that, now, do you?"

Hawks expelled a loud sigh and reluctantly stepped back. Rob quickly moved inside. He looked Hawks squarely in the eyes. "You lied to me, said you were going to call me after you talked to Juan's sister down in Mexico."

"I didn't talk to her. Apparently, the number Juan gave me for her has been disconnected," Hawks said with a shrug. He turned away toward a couch across the room.

Rob followed him, taking a straight-backed chair across from the other man so he could see his face.

"You also told me another lie," Rob said accusingly. "The number you gave me is for the main house, and Lola tells me you don't have a personal phone."

Hawks said harshly, "That woman! She doesn't like me. And I didn't lie to you. I never said I had a phone in my house. Anyone wants to talk to me, they call the main house, and Lola relays the call to me. At least she's supposed to."

Rob stared at him silently for a few moments. All very plausible excuses, yet there was an air of evasiveness about Hawks that bothered Rob. He had the strong feeling that the man was hiding something. Something else Lola said: she said that you always do a disappearing act whenever Mr. Owens is away."

"That's none of your damned business," Hawks snapped. "Or Lola's. I do my job. If I didn't, Mr. Owens would fire me. For your information, things are slow right now. The oranges are ready to pick, but our pickers are all dead. Remember? So until we hire some more, I have little to do. That's what I've been doing the last couple of days, scouring around for a new crew. I finally found one early this morning, so I stopped off to see my woman. You have any objections to that?"

"You're right, Hawks," Rob said. "Your private life is none of my business."

"Speaking of which . . ." Hawks turned his head. "Here she is now. Hi, babe."

Rob looked around. Emerging from the hall behind him was a big, strapping woman around Hawks's age. Where Hawks was dark, she was blond with blue eyes and pale skin. She stopped by Hawks on the couch, her intent gaze on Rob.

Hawks reached out to take her hand. "This is Janice Rust. Janice, I want you to meet Rob Harding."

Rob got to his feet. "I'm glad to meet you, Ms. Rust."

Her murmured words of greeting were lost as Hawks continued, his voice edged with sarcasm. "Mr. Harding is an investigator with the Governor's Task Force on Crime. I'm sure you've heard of that well-known agency seeking out wrongdoers, high and low."

"No, I haven't." She was frowning, her gaze still on Rob. "What've you done, Jed, for him to be investigating you?"

"Nothing, hon," Hawks said airily. "Harding's investigating the murder of Juan Gomez. I told you about that."

"Oh, yes." She finally looked away from Rob and looked down into Hawks's face. "But what do you have to do with that?"

Hawks pulled her down onto the couch beside him. "Why, not a thing, hon." He gave Rob an innocent look. "Isn't that right, Investigator?"

"You're not an active suspect, Hawks, if that's your question." Rob smiled slightly. "But you're not home free, not by a long shot. I have a strong feeling that you aren't telling me all you know, so you'll be seeing me again."

Rob started across the room. Just before he reached the door, he stopped and turned back. "By the way, Hawks, where were you last night? At around ten o'clock, give or take?"

"Why, right here. We were watching a movie on video." Hawks put his arm around Janice's shoulders. "Isn't that right, hon?"

"Yes, that's right, Jed," Janice answered without hesitation. She added defiantly, "Jed was here all night."

Rob nodded. "Good movie?"

"A murder mystery," Hawks said brightly. "The detective in it had a terrible time figuring out who the killer was. In fact, it was his girlfriend who pointed him toward the killer. You got a girlfriend, Investigator?"

Rob's patience was wearing thin. He had an

overpowering urge to stride across the room and clobber the jeering Hawks. He kept a tight rein on his temper and said, "I'm glad you enjoyed the movie, Mr. Hawks. And no, I don't have a girlfriend to help me solve the case. I'll have to do it on my own." He lifted a hand. "You'll be seeing me again, Mr. Hawks."

"I'll be looking forward to it, bro." Hawks's taunting laughter followed Rob out the door.

As he opened the door of the loaner car, his cell phone rang. He picked it up and pressed the button. "Hello?"

It was his supervisor. "Rob, the Border Patrol man I mentioned, Clint Barker, I talked to him a bit ago. He'll be glad to meet with you. He said he'd be having lunch in Sells tomorrow at noon. If you can meet him there, he'll talk to you, fill you in on what he knows, and take you to the spot where they found Juan's body . . ."

CHAPTER 7

It was shortly before noon the next day when Rob drove his repaired pickup into the town of Sells. Sells had a population of around three thousand people and was the center of most reservation activities. There was a hospital; a municipal center, which held the tribal court; the offices of the tribal police department; and various other tribal offices.

The Papago Indian Reservation itself was spread over three million acres, with a population of some ten thousand people.

There were a number of differences between the Papago and the Navajo. Rob had early learned that most non-Native Americans tended to believe that all Native Americans were alike, but this simply wasn't true. There were differences between tribes in language, culture, and even physical appearance.

Much of the difference between the Papago and the

Navajo had to do with the location of their respective reservations. The land where most of the Arizona Navajo lived was dry and not too productive. On the Papago Reservation, the yearly rainfall was also meager, yet wells and irrigation provided needed moisture to the soil. The Papago owned productive farmlands and there was good grazing for cattle.

The Papago also received a rather large income from mining on the reservation. So the Papago, while not wealthy by any means, were better off financially than the Navajo. But in Rob's estimation, the poverty of the Navajo wasn't all that bad. It kept them more isolated, and consequently they clung more to the old gods and the old ways, but perhaps this was not entirely to their detriment. Just reading the daily papers was enough to tell you that the world of the white men, with all of its sophistication, had its own problems.

When Rob reached State Highway 86, he started looking for the restaurant where he was supposed to meet Clint Barker, the Border Patrol agent. It was already ten minutes into the noon hour. Then he spotted it—a family restaurant set back a little from the blare of highway traffic.

Rob parked the pickup and went inside into the welcome coolness of air-conditioning. The restaurant was about half full. Clint Barker was waiting for him in a booth in the rear.

He rose out of the booth to shake Rob's hand. He was tall, well over six feet, and thin as a whippet. His hair was bleached almost white from the desert sun, and his skin was dark as old leather. He was in his mid-forties, Rob estimated.

As they sat down, Barker's gray eyes appraised Rob shrewdly. "I'm curious as to why the task force would be involved in this case."

Rob said, "Well, a crime was committed."

Barker shrugged narrow shoulders. "Even so. Illegals die all the time out here in the desert. According to the statistics, well over a hundred this year by the last count."

"That's one reason right there. There are too many such deaths, and I guess the governor wants something done about it."

Barker shook his head. "It's basically a federal problem, for my people and Immigration."

Rob felt the beginning of a headache. There was almost always a problem of jurisdiction in the cases to which he was assigned. All too often other law enforcement agencies thought that he was stepping onto their turf. Was that the case here?

He said cautiously, "Sometimes there's a problem about just who's in charge."

Barker smiled ruefully. "I know what you mean; all too well, in fact. I've often thought that there ought to be some kind of arbitrator, or some agency to correlate these cases where jurisdiction is contested. I worked one case where the sheriff's office, the local police, and Immigration were all involved, and it was pure hell. Everyone was getting in everyone else's way, and the duplication of effort was ridiculous! This looks like it might be the same."

"Well, that's one of the reasons the task force was formed. The governor feels very strongly about this."

Barker shrugged. "As far as I'm concerned, your being here is fine with me. I have more work than I can handle anyway. I'll take any help I can get. But I can't speak for Immigration or the sheriff's office. Right now, the investigation is being handled by the sheriff's department, and since it happened on Indian land, the FBI will likely be involved, although they haven't shown much interest so far."

"How about the Indian police?"

"I doubt they will get into it," Barker said with a shrug. "Illegals dying out here has become so commonplace that the Indian police pretty much leave it up to other agencies. They're mostly interested in crimes involving their own people."

"There is another difference here," Rob said. "Juan Gomez was murdered. The majority of the deaths of illegals are caused by lack of water and exposure."

"What about the others?"

"As far as I'm concerned, they were all murdered: Gomez first, and then his companions were left to wander out into the desert and die. Do you agree?"

Barker nodded. "Put that way, I suppose you're right. They weren't out there of their own volition. Do you have any leads?"

Rob said cautiously, "Not strong ones. So far, everything points to the coyote."

"Chances are, he's our killer. It's usually the coyote in these cases. Any ideas there?"

"One name keeps cropping up. Juan Gomez has made the trip across every year for some time, and he's always used the same guy—Hoby Macklin. That name ring a bell?"

The gray eyes across from him brightened. "Yeah, I've heard the name. A real piece of work. Macklin's quite active along the border. He's even been busted a couple of times. Both times he skated. It's hard to convict these guys unless they're caught with a load of human cargo. Once they're delivered, the illegals usually won't testify. It's understandable, but it makes our job difficult."

Barker broke off as the waitress came with their orders. Both men had ordered hamburgers and cold drinks. They began to eat. Rob found that he was very hungry, and it was a few moments before he spoke again.

"From all I can learn, they came across at Lukeville, then up through Organ Pipe, and east toward Sells."

Barker nodded. "That seems the most likely scenario."

"The big question seems to be, why was Juan killed and why were the others dumped. Was the Border Patrol or Immigration onto them, maybe chasing them?"

"Not to my knowledge," Barker said with a shake of his head. "Certainly none of my people were chasing a coyote vehicle. I asked a guy with Immigration, and he said no."

"The sheriff's people?"

"Not that I heard. And that wouldn't be likely. A sheriff's vehicle might have witnessed a traffic violation and given chase, but not for smuggling illegals. That's not their job unless they're radioed by us for help."

Rob's voice burned with frustration. "Then why in the hell would the coyote kill his passengers unless he'd been spotted? He'd be throwing away his chance of getting the rest of his money on delivery."

"Most of these guys demand all their money in advance, Harding."

"I know that. But Juan Gomez was an old hand. I think he would have paid half off the top, the other half on delivery."

"That's possible. But think about this." Barker leaned forward, his voice soft. "If Gomez had worked it that way, where would the second half of the dough have to be?"

"What difference . . . ?" Rob broke off. "Of course, he'd have to be carrying it on him."

"Exactly. So if they whacked him out there, they'd still get their money."

"Which brings up the question: did Juan have any money on his person?"

"A few pesos, small change, no big money."

Rob, deep in thought, finished the last bite of his burger and took the last swallow of his cold drink. "There is one thing . . . I've learned that Gomez was thinking of using another coyote the next time. It seems he'd lost trust in Macklin."

"Any reason?"

Rob shook his head. "Nope, he was secretive about that for some reason."

"There you go!" Barker rapped the table with his knuckles. "Macklin found out and decided to kill this Gomez. Maybe Gomez had something on him and Macklin was afraid he'd go to the law."

"That's always possible," Rob said slowly. "But somehow it doesn't feel right. It seems there has to be something more than that."

Barker grinned faintly. "That old cop hunch, eh? We all get 'em. But you know something? I've learned from long experience that they're on the money only about half the time. How about you?"

"Yeah." Rob laughed. "Maybe less than half with me." He changed tack. "I read a copy of your report, Clint. I gather that you didn't find the body?"

"Nope," Barker said with a shake of his head. "Some tourist spotted the body early in the morning and called the sheriff's office. We got the word later, and I drove out from our office in Tucson. The body was still there when I arrived."

"Do you have time today to take me to the location?"

"Sure," Barker said with a shrug. "But I don't know

what you hope to find. The crime scene has been gone over thoroughly."

"Probably nothing, but I always like to look at the scene." Rob shifted embarrassedly. "Sometimes . . . Well, hell, sometimes I get a feeling for what happened. Indulge me, okay?"

"Sure." Barker grinned. "Maybe you'll get one of your 'feelings' and solve the whole thing right there."

Rob laughed shortly. "Don't bet on it. We were talking a moment ago about no money found in Juan's pockets?"

"Yeah, that's right."

Rob felt frustration gnaw at him. "That must mean he paid in advance, which strikes me as strange. Especially since he was thinking of using another coyote."

"Like I said, the coyote could have looted Juan's pockets after shooting him."

"That had occurred to me, but . . ." Rob waved a hand. "According to your report, the bullet that killed Juan was fired from a .38 revolver?"

"Right, .38 caliber. Now all we have to do is find the weapon and we can match it up." Barker sighed. "Fat chance of that, to my way of thinking."

"You're probably right," Rob said glumly.

A few minutes later they walked out of the cafe together. Outside, Barker said, "The way it's usually handled, the coyote collects his money from the person who is employing the illegals." He glanced over at Rob. "Unless they were coming over looking for work?"

"No, no." Rob shook his head. "They had work already lined up. Juan had worked seasonally for years for Thad Owens, up near Phoenix, in his orange grove. And Owens does it differently than most growers. He sends the money to Juan every year to pay the coyote. Juan recruited the additional workers and got them across. Apparently, Owens didn't want any personal contact with the coyote."

Barker said, "That's a little unusual, trusting an illegal with the money." He chuckled. "Maybe you shouldn't have told me about Owens. I could bust him for employing illegal aliens."

"Never stick," Rob said with a shake of his head. "Owens does it all secondhand, no way of tracing it back to him."

Barker laughed. "I wasn't about to do it, anyway. I have enough on my plate."

They stopped by a vehicle with the Border Patrol logo on the side. Barker said, "You want to leave your transportation here and ride out and back with me? It's about an hour's drive."

Rob hesitated briefly. "No, I'd better take my own pickup. I'm not sure where I'll go afterward."

"Suit yourself. Follow me then."

There wasn't a lot of traffic on the highway heading west, and Rob had no trouble following the Border Patrol vehicle. He drove more or less on autopilot, his mind engaged. This was the most difficult case he had been involved in since joining the force. There was no real focus to it. Some of his other cases had been hard, but at least he had been able to home in on the chief elements.

Not so this time. There were so many elements that every time he focused on one, it wandered off in several directions. Perhaps it was because the case spread across half of the state of Arizona. Worse, it even spread into Mexico. For the first time, Rob wondered if he would have to eventually venture into Mexico before he could find all the answers. Maybe he would even have to go deep into Mexico, to Juan's hometown. A talk with his wife, his sister, might help clarify some things.

About an hour's drive out of Sells, Barker's vehicle began to slow, and his right turn signal started flashing. A few minutes later he pulled off the highway onto a turnout. Rob followed him in and parked behind the Border Patrol vehicle.

As Rob shut off the motor and got out, he caught a glimpse of a van flashing past on the highway.

Rob stared at it. It was a black van. Even as he stared, it was picking up more speed, already fifty yards down the road. It was too far away to get a good look at the license plate. Was it smeared with mud? He couldn't tell for certain.

"Naw, it couldn't be," he said aloud and turned away.

As he walked toward Clint Barker, Rob surveyed the area. The ground was covered with gravel. It wouldn't show tire tracks, Rob thought. On each side of the highway, the desert seemed to stretch into infinity. There were no buildings in sight. To the north, almost hidden in the heat haze, was a range of low mountains. To the south, dark thunderclouds were piling themselves into a formidable-looking black wall. A monsoon storm was traveling fast toward them. Rob heard a rumble of thunder like distant cannon fire.

The air was growing humid, and Rob felt sweat running down his spine. He met Barker halfway between the two vehicles.

He said, "This is the spot?"

"Yeah." Barker pointed to the edge of the gravel. "Gomez's body was found over there. I'd say he wasn't even given a chance to run, gunned down as he got out of the truck or whatever he was in."

"Van," Rob said absently. "At least, Macklin uses a van to transport his illegals across the border."

Rob walked over to the spot indicated. There was nothing to see, of course, not even any sign of blood.

Barker said, "Since Gomez was the only one shot, it would seem reasonable to assume that he was the prime target. Maybe they couldn't have gotten all the others, but one at least, maybe more, if they wanted to kill them."

Rob nodded agreement. "Yes, I'm sure Juan was the targeted victim. The others were just incidental." He gazed off into the desert. "Where were the bodies found, which side of the highway?"

"Both sides," Barker said. "Three to the north, about five miles in. The other was found to the south. Poor guy only made a couple of miles before he died."

Rob closed his eyes tightly and stood silently for several moments. He had never made any claim to having psychic powers, yet often he could visualize parts of what had happened at a crime scene. This wasn't unusual, he knew. Many veteran homicide officers could do that. The picture was never complete. It came in fragments, like bits of a jigsaw puzzle scattered about.

Suddenly, in his vision, a black van roared up, stopping with a spray of gravel under braking wheels. It was so real, so vivid, that Rob's eyes flew open. He stared at the spot where the van should have been.

There was nothing there, of course.

Barker said in alarm, "You all right, Rob? You look like you've seen a ghost."

"Something like that," Rob muttered.

He closed his eyes again. But the mood, the psychic connection, whatever it was, was gone, shattered.

Rob well realized that he could have conjured the black van up out of nothing. He could have been influenced by the van that had haunted him the past two days. He had even thought that the same van had been following him to this spot . . .

He shook his head clear of such thoughts. The sun suddenly disappeared behind a cloud. Lightning forked the sky, followed by a crack of thunder. To the south, less than a mile away, a dark curtain of rain connected the clouds to the ground.

Barker said, "No feelings, no vibes?"

Rob shook his head. "Some strange feelings, yeah. But I'm afraid no sudden insights toward a solution." He glanced around. "But I'm glad I came out. Thanks for coming along, Clint."

"That's okay, Rob, but I have to be getting back to Tucson. I have to hit the office before the end of the day." He gestured to the approaching rain. "Looks like we're in for a good one. It's going to slow down the driving."

"You go along," Rob said with a nod. "I'll head out too."

Rob lingered for a bit after Barker drove away. He walked over to the spot where Juan's body had been found. Again, he closed his eyes and tried to call up a flash of the crime. Nothing came. His head began to ache.

The first drops of water struck him. Big, fat drops. He opened his eyes. The day had darkened until it was almost twilight. He hurried to his pickup and got in. The wind had come up, and it blew the rain in sheets across his windshield. He had to stop for a few moments to let two cars coming from the west pass on by. The two vehicles were traveling close together. The second one was almost riding the bumper of the lead vehicle.

The second vehicle was a black van!

Rob pulled onto the highway with a screech of tires. He accelerated. The van was a hundred yards down the road now. Rob's heart pounded in his chest. He focused on the van to the exclusion of everything else. In minutes he was only yards from the vehicle. He could see the license plate clearly. He committed the numbers to memory.

A few months back Stanley Morgan had purchased revolving red lights for his investigators to clamp on the roofs of their vehicles should the need arise. Rob reached into the glove compartment for his. He stretched his arm outside and clamped the light to the roof above his head. He switched it on. The light began to revolve, throwing streaks of red light into the darkening day.

Then he picked up his cell phone to call Mary Sue and have her check on the number.

No!

He slammed the phone back down. The memory of the attack by the van driver the other night flooded his mind. His rage vaulted. A warning bell rang far back in his mind, but he ignored it.

He pounded on the horn, a constant blare of sound. He stuck his hand out the window and waved at the driver to pull over. They continued like that, pickup and van almost bumper to bumper, for a half mile.

Then the van's taillights flashed red, and it began to slow. It pulled over to the side of the road. Rob parked the pickup behind it and got out.

Belatedly, a nudge of caution caused him to approach the van carefully, fully alert now. If this was the van and the driver had a gun . . .

But he kept doggedly on. As he edged close to the driver's door, he held himself ready to chop down on an arm coming out of the window with a gun. Then he was there. He took a final step and looked into the cab.

A pale, frightened face looked out at him. The driver was a boy. He couldn't be more than seventeen, and he looked frightened to death.

"What is it, mister?" a quavering voice said. "What did I do?"

Rob's anger collapsed, leaking from him like air from a pricked balloon. It took a moment to find his voice. Finally he said, "It's a mistake, son. You're not the one I'm looking for. I'm sorry if I frightened you."

He stepped back and waved the van on. The van drove away, slowly at first, then picking up speed. The rain pounding down on his bare head, Rob stared after it.

He felt like an idiot. He had made a complete fool of himself. He knew that this case was getting under his skin, but there was no excuse for what he had just done. If the driver had been who Rob thought, he could easily have killed Rob. Even more importantly, he, an experienced investigator, had acted like the greenest rookie, allowing his emotions to rule his common sense.

He turned and trudged back to the pickup in the driving rain. He removed the light from the cab roof. Drained and suddenly exhausted from the overload of adrenaline, it took him a few minutes to collect himself and drive on.

CHAPTER
8

The storm followed Rob most of the way back to Phoenix, and he wasn't able to get the task force office on his cell phone. By the time he was back in the greater Phoenix area, the lightning and the wind had subsided enough that he was able to get through.

He got Mary Sue in Research on the line first. "Any luck in tracking down Hoby Macklin?"

"Sorry, sugar," she said in her soft, Southern drawl. "The guy seems to have fallen off the face of the earth."

"Damn it! There must be a vehicle registered to him!" Rob said in frustration.

"Not under the name Hoby Macklin. He's probably using another name, Rob," she said. "What's more, I can't trace him back farther than Phoenix. He seems to have appeared out of nowhere, then disappeared the same way."

"His prints must be on file. He was arrested a couple of times."

"Oh, yes, he's been printed, and I'm trying track his prints back to before he came here. I've sent them to the FBI, but you know how slow they are to respond. Smuggling aliens across the border isn't high on their list of priorities."

Rob sighed. "Seems to me that murder falls into the high-priority category, but keep at it."

"I fully intend to, Mr. Harding," Mary Sue said tartly.

"Sorry, Mary Sue. I've had a bad day. Will you connect me with the boss now?"

"Will do."

"Thanks, Mary Sue."

A moment later Rob was talking to Stanley Morgan.

"Learn anything at the site, Rob?" Morgan asked.

"Nothing that will be much help, I'm afraid."

"How did it go with the Border Patrol guy?"

"Barker was most cooperative," Rob said. "Most of all, he didn't seem to resent us entering the case."

"That's a switch, isn't it?" Morgan said with a chuckle. "Who knows, maybe someday soon we'll be considered equal to all the other law enforcement branches."

Rob took a few minutes to fill his supervisor in on what had happened since he had talked to him last. He omitted only one detail—his abortive chase-down of the black van. Usually when reporting to Morgan, he omitted nothing, not even any mistakes he might have made, but this one was too humiliating. Every time he thought of that episode he felt a flush of shame at his juvenile behavior.

Neither did he tell Morgan about the psychic flash he had experienced at the scene of the murder of Juan Gomez—if that was what it was. He well knew that the supervisor was highly skeptical about such things.

Morgan believed only in hard, cold facts.

When he was finished with his report, Rob said, "How about Thad Owens? Did you have a chat with him?"

"Yes, I had dinner with him last night," Morgan said with a chuckle. "I waited until he had a few under his belt, then told him that you thought he wasn't being very cooperative. He got indignant, swore that that wasn't true. But he finally admitted that he might not have been as forthcoming as he could have been.

"At any rate, he agreed to see you again. He said he'd be at home all morning. It seems that he got a replacement crew to pick his fruit and will be overseeing getting them started. Can you make it in the morning?"

"No problem," Rob replied. "I'll drive up early."

"Rob," Morgan began, then paused for a moment to clear his throat. "Do you think he might somehow be involved in all this?"

"I have no reason to think so, but I do think he knows more than he was telling me. For instance, it doesn't make sense that he doesn't know about Hoby Macklin, and it appears more and more that Macklin is the key."

Morgan hesitated again. "The reason I asked the question is, if Owens is in any way involved, come down on him hard. Just because Thad is a friend of mine doesn't in any way mean that you should go easy on him. If a friend of mine is involved in a crime, friendship goes out the window. Is that understood, Rob?"

"Understood, sir, but I'm sure it won't come to that."

"I hope not. But one of the rules I live by is: people may disappoint me, but they seldom surprise me."

*   *   *

Rob arrived at the Owens place shortly after nine the next morning. As he drove slowly down the road between the orderly rows of orange trees, he heard voices chattering in Spanish off to his right. He parked the pickup off the road and started walking toward the sound of the voices. The odor of oranges was strong in his nostrils. He knew that a certain number of oranges were dropped and bruised, no matter how careful the pickers were.

About a hundred yards into the grove, he came upon a scene of activity. Six pickers were at work on the trees; four workers were on the ground, plucking the oranges from the lower branches, and two were on stepladders, working the upper branches.

Thad Owens stood off to one side, a cigar fuming between his lips. There was a look of satisfaction on his face. Jed Hawks stood beside a small truck loaded with bins. As Rob watched, one picker approached the truck with a full sack hanging from his shoulder. He removed the sack and dumped the oranges into a bin.

Hawks said in a scolding voice, "Careful there, don't bruise them!"

The picker, who looked Mexican, ignored him. *Probably doesn't understand a word of English*, Rob thought.

He stopped beside Owens, who looked at him with a scowl. He motioned at the retreating man. "See how much I miss Juan? This bunch are hit and miss, don't care how the work is done, just so they put in their hours and get paid. Worse, not a one of them speaks a damned word of English!"

Rob decided on the instant to risk the man's anger. He said, "You'd think as long as Hawks has been working around Hispanics he'd have learned how to communicate with them."

"Never had to worry about it before," Owens said with a shrug. "Juan was always here at picking time."

"Seems to me the best move would be to hire a foreman who speaks Spanish."

Owens swung on him angrily. "What is this, Harding? You're supposed to be investigating Juan's murder, not telling me how to run my business!"

Rob sensed that there was something a little off about the relationship between Owens and Jed Hawks. It obviously went beyond employer-employee, but he decided that he had pushed it far enough for the moment. He said, "Sorry, it was just an idle comment. I wasn't trying to tell you how to run your business."

"Sure sounded like it to me," Owens said in a growling voice. "I promised Stanley I'd cooperate with you, but if you keep this up, you can vacate my property right now!"

Rob held up a hand. "Again, my apologies, Mr. Owens. You're right; it's none of my business."

Owens subsided, still grumbling. "Don't know what I can tell you, anyway. Told you everything I know the first time you were here."

"Perhaps, perhaps not." Rob paused for a moment. Hawks had noticed his presence and stood staring. He was clearly nervous and worried. What was he worried about? Was he afraid that Owens might reveal something?

"Well?" Owens said in that same growling voice.

"You told me that Juan Gomez had worked for you for . . . ten years, I believe you said?"

"Something like that, yes."

"And every year he would call you from across the border, and you would discuss how many workers you'd need. Then he'd hire the workers, and you'd send him the money to pay the coyote?"

Owens grunted. "That's about says it, yeah."

"From my understanding, the way it's usually done, the

grower usually pays the fare on this end, or at least the last half of it."

"I learned to trust Juan," Owens said heavily.

"What you're really saying, Mr. Owens, is that you wanted no personal contact with the coyote. You wanted it all done at one remove, keep your hands clean. Isn't that correct, Mr. Owens?"

Owens glared at him balefully. "What gives you the right to talk to me like that?" Then he turned away, shoulders slumping. "All right, have it your own way, lad. Yeah, that's the way I handled it. Not that I think there's anything wrong with hiring illegals, but I have a position to maintain, a reputation. I can't afford to be dragged into court over some piddling thing like that!"

Rob was silent for a few moments before saying, "I know I asked this question before, but I'll ask it again. You told me you had never met Juan's coyote."

"That's correct." Owens grinned slyly. "As the saying goes, I had no need to know."

"His name is Hoby Macklin. Ever heard the name?"

Owens frowned in thought. "Hoby's an unusual name. It seems that I may have heard it before, but I'm not sure in what connection."

"But not from Juan?" Rob said quickly.

Owens gave a shrug. "May have been Juan, but I couldn't swear to it."

"Someone tried to kill me the other night, Mr. Owens. I have reason to believe it may have been Hoby Macklin."

Owens made a whistling sound. "Now why would he do that, lad?"

"The only reason I can think of is that he believes that I'm close to solving the case."

"Well, now, that's to the good, isn't it? That would mean he did kill Juan." Then Owens frowned. "Of course, that's not so good for you, is it, lad? Puts you in harm's way, you might say."

"Hazards of the job," Rob said and realized it was a rather pompous statement. He said, "Did you know that Juan had a sister, name of Linda?"

"Sure, I talked to her the day after Juan was murdered."

Rob stared at him in astonishment. "You did? Why didn't you mention it to me?"

Owens gave one of his shrugs. "You didn't ask and I didn't think it was important. How could the sister have anything to do with Juan's death? The only reason I called was to inform her about what had happened to her brother. Juan had given me her number, said his own household didn't have a phone."

"How did she take the news?"

Owens said, "Not very well. What would you expect?"

"Hawks told me it was his job to call her."

Owens looked off toward where Hawks stood. "I don't know why he said that. He can't speak the language, as you just saw."

"A woman in our office tried to find a phone number for Linda Gomez and was told that she had no phone."

"Probably got wrong information. You know how screwed up those people are down there."

Rob asked, "Did she say she was coming up to the States?"

"Nope, didn't mention it to me. I'm making arrangements to ship the body down there as soon as the coroner's office releases it. I called, and they promised to release it in a couple more days." Owens grimaced. "But then you know how bureaucrats are.

Might be a couple of days, might be a week . . ."

He was interrupted by a voice raised in anger. Both men glanced toward the sound. It was Jed Hawks. Flushed darkly, he had one of the workers by the shirtfront and was shaking the man violently.

With Rob in the lead, the two watchers started toward the scene. As they reached it, Hawks flung the worker away. The man stumbled and fell onto his back. He lay staring up at Hawks in fear.

Owens barked, "What's going on here, Jed?"

Hawks turned, fuming. "He dumped a whole sack of fruit into the bin like marbles. Bruised the oranges. We're probably going to have to toss them! I don't know why these guys don't learn to speak English before they come up here to work."

Rob said, "Seems to me it'd be useful to you to learn to speak enough of their language to communicate."

Hawks glared. "Who asked you, Harding? This is none of your business."

Owens waved them both quiet. In a low voice he said, "I agree with you, Jed. But don't forget how hard it was to find pickers on such short notice. You stir these guys up and they walk, my fruit may fall off the trees before we put together another crew. So go easy, okay?"

Hawks turned his glare on the grove owner. For a moment Rob thought the foreman was going to talk back to his boss. He sensed that it had happened before, and again he had to wonder how Hawks could get away with such insolence and still hold his job.

Owens said, "Walk it off, Jed. Cool off before you come back. I'll keep an eye on them meanwhile. Now go on; get a rein on that temper of yours."

The tension between employer and employee was

almost strong enough to touch. Then Hawks grunted deep in his throat and turned on his heel. Shoulders held rigid as boards, he strode off.

Rob stood undecided for a long moment. He needed to question Hawks. He had learned that often people were more likely to answer questions when angry and upset. He said, "Excuse me for a few minutes, Mr. Owens. I'll be back."

Owens grinned tightly. "I'll be here, lad. I promised Stanley I'd answer all your questions to the best of my ability."

Rob hurried after Hawks. He caught up with him just as he reached the road and turned toward the house, walking fast.

Rob touched him on the elbow. "Hawks . . ."

Hawks turned toward him, a snarl on his face. "What?"

"I have a few questions."

"Questions! Always with the questions. The first words you spoke as a baby must have been a question!" But he slowed to a more normal pace. "Ask them quickly then, because I have to get away from this place for a while before I hit somebody."

"You lied to me about Linda Gomez. You said it was your job to inform her of Juan's death. Yet Mr. Owens tells me that he did that, the day Juan was found murdered."

Hawks stopped, shooting Rob a look of surprise. "He did? Funny, he didn't mention that to me. Nasty job like that he usually leaves to me."

"He also said that you wouldn't be doing it because you don't speak Spanish."

Hawks grinned wolfishly. "That's where he's wrong. Linda speaks better English than I do. Juan told me that when he gave me her number."

"There's another thing. You told me that you were the one Juan normallly called for instructions before crossing the border, and that you talked to Juan just before he was killed."

Hawks frowned. "So?"

"Well, Mr. Owens told me that he was the one who talked to Juan and gave him his instructions."

"I can explain that," Hawks said with a careless shrug. "Juan talked to both of us. He talked to Mr. Owens the first time because I wasn't here when he called."

Rob stared at him. "You have an answer for everything, don't you, Hawks?"

Hawks's smile was edged with insolence. "That's what you want, isn't it, answers to your questions?"

"The right answers, yeah."

"I've been giving you the right answers, bro. You say I've been lying to you." He added challengingly, "Prove it!"

"I intend to," Rob said grimly. "And if I catch you in another lie, Hawks, you'll be facing an obstruction of justice charge."

"Oh, I'm scared, Harding," Hawks said mockingly. "Now, if that's all . . ."

"One more question: have you heard from Carlos?"

"Not a word. What's that saying, 'vanished into thin air'? Yeah, that's it," Hawks said with a nod.

"Doesn't that strike you as strange?"

"Lots of things in the white man's world strike me as strange, bro," Hawks said with a dry laugh. "Can't let it bother me too much. Now, if you're through with me, I have a place to go and things to do."

Rob made a vague gesture and then stood watching Hawks stride away. Was Hawks really leaving the property? Rob stepped back into the grove and waited. In a few minutes he heard the sound of a vehicle coming from the direction of the house. An almost new pickup came down the road, moving fast. Rob had a glimpse of Hawks behind the wheel.

How could Hawks just leave in the middle of fruit picking, the busiest time of the year for orange growers? Sure, Owens had told him to take a walk and cool down, but just drive off the ranch?

Rob had no answers.

He walked back into the grove and to where Owens stood by the truck holding the bins. He was smoking a big cigar and watching the pickers.

Rob said, "I'm getting two different stories here, Mr. Owens. Hawks tells me that he was the person Juan talked to just before he returned every year. Yet you did it this time. Why is that?"

"Simple. Hawks wasn't around when Juan called, so I handled it. Juan did call a second time, and Hawks talked to him then."

"You know, it seems to me that Hawks goes and comes as he pleases. He drove off the property just now, right in the middle of the picking. Most fruit ranchers wouldn't allow their foreman to do that. Why do you?"

Rob was expecting an explosion of temper, but Owens merely smiled. He said genially, "Jed and me go back a ways. I knew him long before he came to work for me. Matter of fact, his daddy worked for me when I was just starting these groves. So I reckon ours is more than just an employer-employee relationship."

Rob was far from satisfied with the answer, but he realized that he wasn't going to get any more out of this man at the moment.

Owens had fallen silent, watching the pickers at work. Now he spoke again. "Lad, I hope I've answered all your questions to your satisfaction this time. For I sure as hell want you to catch that van-driving scum who murdered poor Juan. Juan was the best worker I ever had, a man who wouldn't harm a fly. Everybody liked him."

"Seems somebody didn't, Mr. Owens," Rob said dryly.

Owens looked around at him. "Maybe not. Maybe Juan wasn't the target. There were others involved. Maybe Juan just happened to be in the way and caught a bullet meant for somebody else."

"I don't see it that way, Mr. Owens. I think Juan was the target all the way," Rob said grimly. "The why I don't know yet, but I will eventually. Thank you for your cooperation."

He held out his hand and they shook.

"Glad to do all I can, lad, but I fail to see how I was much more help than the first time."

*   *   *

Halfway back to Phoenix, Rob felt a concern gnawing at the edges of his mind.

Something had been said this morning during his conversations with either Thad Owens or Jed Hawks that was off-key. What was it?

Or was it something that hadn't been said?

He worried over it all the way back to his apartment, but the thought wouldn't emerge into the light of day so he could examine it. He knew from experience that, whatever it was, it would become clear with time. The best way to handle something like that was to let it lurk back there in his mind until the time was right.

CHAPTER 9

Rob wanted to call Mary Sue in Research, but it was the noon hour by the time he got back to the Phoenix area, and Mary Sue would be out to lunch.

He waited until he was back in his apartment and at his small desk in a corner of the living room before calling. When he got her on the phone, he said, "Mary Sue, it's Rob Harding."

"Well, Investigator Harding!" she said brightly. "How are you today? And to answer your first question, no, I'm still coming up zilch on Hoby Macklin. You sure that he even exists?"

He said, "I'm reasonably sure there's a coyote out there that I desperately need to talk to, but what if Hoby Macklin is an assumed name? What if he has a past history under another name?"

"Now that is more than possible," she replied. "Hoby

Macklin even sounds like an alias."

"I don't suppose you've heard back from the fingerprint check with the FBI?"

"Nope, not yet. Tell you what, I'll give them a call right now. There's a problem here." She sighed. "The task force doesn't have much creditability yet. There's even some animosity between the bureau and the task force. Our investigators have been involved in cases that the FBI considers we have no business nosing into."

"I know," Rob said glumly. "That may happen with this case. Juan Gomez apparently was killed on reservation land—at least, his body was dumped there. That puts the murder under FBI jurisdiction. The Border Patrol guy I saw yesterday said they haven't been showing much interest in the case as yet. That may change."

Mary Sue said, "I'll see if I can rattle a few cages, Rob."

"There're a couple of other people I'd like you to check on, Mary Sue. Jed Hawks and Thad Owens."

"Thad Owens, I'm familiar with. Pretty important guy to be checking on, isn't he, Rob?"

"Yes, he is, and he's also the boss's friend, but Mr. Morgan told me not to let that interfere with my investigation. I'm not saying Owens is a suspect, not at all; I'd just like some general background information."

"And the other one, Jed Hawks?"

"Hawks works for Owens, supervising his orange grove," Rob said. "Dig up whatever you can on him, Mary Sue."

"Will do."

"Thanks, I appreciate it." Rob took a deep breath. "Now, another thing, the matter of the telephone number for Linda Gomez down in Mexico. I'm getting conflicting stories on that. You tell me that the telephone company said she didn't have a phone. Yet Thad Owens told me that he talked to her the day after Juan was killed."

"That does seem odd, Rob. Maybe Owens is lying."

Rob laughed shortly. "That's always possible. It seems everybody is lying to me in this case. But why would he do that? He has to know that I would find out."

"Well, I'll call down there again. Like I said, I became friendly with a phone operator with Telmex. Actually, Rob, I fail to see why it's all that important."

"I need to talk to Linda Gomez, for several reasons. I may end up going down there, if for nothing else but to walk in Juan's shoes. And see if you can get the FBI to move on Macklin's prints. . . . Wait a minute, I just thought of something. Hold off on that until I get back to you, Mary Sue."

He punched out and left the apartment. He got into his pickup and drove across town to the hardware store where Steve Brack worked.

Brack was with a customer when Rob came in. He appeared alarmed when he spotted Rob. Rob motioned for Brack to continue with his customer and hung back until Brack was free.

"What are you doing here?" Brack said in a whisper. He raked the large room with a fearful glance. "You said you were through with me. If my boss sees you talking to me . . ."

Rob took Brack's arm in a strong grip and squeezed. "You lied to me!"

Brack winced and tried to pull away. "You're hurting me, and I didn't lie to you, I swear!"

"Is there somewhere we can talk for a minute?"

Brack's face assumed a stubborn look.

Rob added in a louder voice, "Either you talk to me

or I call your boss over and tell him who I am and why I'm here."

"You told me I wasn't a suspect!"

Rob smiled wolfishly. "That's what I said then; now it's different. Do we talk or not?"

Brack's shoulders slumped. With his head he motioned toward the back. "Back here."

Rob followed the man into the back of the store. Most of the huge back room was taken up with hardware items of every sort. Brack went to a door in one corner and opened it.

"We can talk here," he said in a low voice. "There's nobody here at the moment."

They entered the room, and Brack closed the door. The room was a break room with a table and several chairs. A small refrigerator sat on a counter holding a sink and a coffeemaker.

Brack faced him. "I didn't lie to you, Mr. Harding!"

"By omission you did," Rob said relentlessly.

Brack took a step back. "What do you mean?"

"You told me that you and Macklin had known each other for years. But Macklin isn't his real name, is it? He was born and grew up with another name." Rob took a threatening step forward. "Didn't he?"

Brack said defiantly, "I don't know what you mean!"

"Yes, you do. I want that name. If you don't give it to me, you're in a world of trouble. By withholding information about a crime, you face an obstruction of justice charge. If that happens, you could go to jail. The very least that could happen would be that you would lose your job here."

Brack threw up his hands. "All right, all right! I'll tell

you. His real name is Tobe Marvin." He laughed without humor. "I don't know how many times Tobe's changed his name over the years. Every time he gets into trouble he changes his identity, has papers made up. He changes like a . . . What do they call that lizard?"

"A chameleon?"

"Yes, that's it!" Brack bobbed his head.

Rob said, "Since he's in deep trouble now, the odds are good that he's changed his name again, isn't it?"

Brack bobbed his head again. "Yeah, it is. But I don't know that for sure, I swear. If he's using a new name, I don't know it."

Rob had a thought. "When he makes these changes of identity, does he get a new vehicle to conduct his coyote business?"

Brack nodded. "Yes."

"Usually another van?"

"Every time. He may change the color and make, but it's always a van."

Rob thought for a moment, staring directly into Brack's eyes. He had the sense that Brack was holding nothing back this time.

Brack said nervously, "My boss is going to start wondering why I'm back here so long. We're not supposed to take breaks longer than fifteen minutes."

"Okay, you can go back to work. Wait . . ." Rob held up a hand. "If you've told me everything this time, you'll never see me again, Mr. Brack. But I find out you've lied to me, you're in deep trouble."

Brack said vehemently, "The truth, all the way."

*   *   *

A few blocks away from the hardware store, Rob pulled

to the curb and punched out the number for Research on his cell phone. When he got Mary Sue, he said without preamble, "The name we want is Tobe Marvin."

"What?" Mary Sue said in confusion.

"Sorry. Hoby Macklin's real name, his birth name, is Tobe Marvin." He went on to tell her what he had learned from Brack. "See what you can find under that name, Mary Sue. I don't know if that'll help us find him, but it might."

"Okay, Rob," she said. "I'll get right on it."

When Rob got home, his desk phone was ringing. He snatched it up. "Hello?"

A voice with a Spanish accent said tentatively, "Rob Harding?"

"Yes, this Rob Harding."

"This is Carlos Ramos . . ."

Rob felt a quickening of interest. At last!

He said, "Hello, Carlos. I'm glad to . . ."

Carlos interrupted, "Are you the man who visited my mother, asking about me? The man who left his card?"

"That's right, Carlos. Why did you run from me in that orchard? Why have you been hiding?"

Once again, Carlos interrupted, "No questions now. Not on the telephone. Will you meet with me, Señor Harding?"

"Yes, of course. Where?"

"At my mother's house. You know where it is—you were there."

"I know where it is, sure, but do you want to involve your mother in this?"

"My mother will not be there. She does work for the

church three evenings a week. I will drive her there, and we will be alone in her house. Eight o'clock this evening. Please be on time, Señor Harding."

"Wait, Carlos . . ."

But all Rob heard was the hum of an empty line.

Rob sat for a while, musing. Was this the break he had been hoping for? It was clear that Carlos knew something; that had to be the reason he had been in hiding. Maybe he knew the answers to all the questions.

Rob well knew the old police rule: never go to a meeting with an informant or a suspect without backup. Stanley Morgan had belabored the point many times; a call like this could easily be a trap.

Rob shook his head. No one would use his own mother's house to set a trap where violence might take place. The only thing that bothered Rob was the time element. It was now only the middle of the afternoon; he had hours to wait before the meeting.

Even as he pondered the situation, the phone rang. He scooped up the receiver. "Hello?"

"Rob?" It was Mary Sue. "I just got through talking with my new friend at Telmex in Mexico."

"Good! What did you find out?"

"Linda Gomez did have a telephone. But she had it disconnected the day after her brother was found shot."

"And I suppose no phone in her name was taken out somewhere else?"

"Nope," Mary Sue said. "Not as far as my friend knows."

"Thanks anyway, Mary Sue."

"You're welcome," Mary Sue said. "Too early yet to report anything on your new name, Tobe Marvin. The check on Owens and Hawks is ongoing. Should have a report for you on that soon."

*   *   *

On the theory that it always pays to be early for a rendezvous with an informant, Rob planned to arrive at the Ramos house at least thirty minutes early.

Driving across town took awhile. It might be he was afflicted with a raging case of paranoia, but people seemed to have a way of knowing where he was at any given time. So it was entirely possible that he was being followed.

Unfortunately, he hit the tail end of the going-home traffic tangle when he started out. There was heavy traffic everywhere, which made it very easy to follow him. He employed all the tried-and-true maneuvers. He made sudden turns, always keeping an eye in his rearview mirror for a tail, for a vehicle that made the turns with him.

Once, he was sure he spotted a black van behind him. He slowed down, getting into the curb lane. A few minutes later the van sailed past him in the passing lane. It was a dark gray in color and had a woman driver.

With a rueful shake of his head, Rob drove on. He got on and off I-17 three times. Finally, in Chandler, he pulled into a convenience-store parking lot and sat for fifteen minutes. Vehicles stopped but left soon afterwards. Since no parking was allowed on the street, it would have been extremely difficult for anyone to have him under surveillance.

Finally, satisfied that he hadn't been followed, he pulled out into the traffic again. It was just dark when he reached the block where the Ramos residence was located. Lights were on in most of the houses on the block, and TVs were blaring. It was past the rush hour now; most people were home and relaxing before dinner.

There was parking on the street, and a number of

vehicles were already parked, including a motorcycle almost directly in front of the house. Rob found a slot four doors down and parked the pickup. He was able to see the house; at the moment it was dark.

Ten minutes after he parked, a dusty sedan, several years old, pulled into the Ramos driveway. A man Rob recognized as the person he had talked to briefly in the Owens grove got out and went into the house.

Rob sat on, watchful. There was still ten minutes before he was expected, and he wanted to see if anyone else was watching the house. Or if anyone else went in.

Suddenly, a muffled sound alerted him. Had it come from the Ramos house? It sounded like a gunshot, or could it have come from some TV program from one of the houses?

Rob leaned forward as the door to the Ramos house opened, and a man hurried out. The man wore a motorcycle helmet that obscured his face.

Without further hesitation Rob exited the pickup. He started at a dead run toward the Ramos house just as the motorcycle parked in front roared to life and pulled away from the curb with a screech of tires. Rob was too far away to get a good look at the license plate. The motorcycle accelerated and was nearing the corner before Rob reached the spot where it had been parked. Now it turned the corner and was out of sight.

Rob stopped running, half-turning back toward his pickup. Should he set out in pursuit of the motorcycle? But he was now sure that the sound he had heard had been a gunshot. He ran toward the house.

As he went up the walk, he saw that the front door stood partly open, light spilling out. He stopped at the door, pushing it open with his toe.

"Mr. Ramos? Carlos Ramos, are you in there?"

There was no response. With a cold feeling in his belly, he warily entered, stepping directly into a short hallway leading toward the rear of the house. It was empty; the only light came from a room in the back. Rob judged that the room was the kitchen.

He called again, "Mr. Ramos? This is Rob Harding."

Again there was no answer.

His dread mounting, Rob cautiously stepped into the brightly lit kitchen. It was empty. Where was Carlos? Was he dead somewhere else in the house?

Then Rob saw the door at the back of the kitchen. It was open. Rob started toward it. He was halfway across the room when he saw the blood spots on the linoleum floor. The spots made a trail leading through the door.

There was a light switch on the wall by the door. Rob thumbed it on, and the backyard flooded with light. There was a small stoop just outside the door. Rob stood on it, looking carefully around the yard. It was also empty. There was a wire fence across the back with an open gate.

Rob stepped down into the yard and started toward the gate, his gaze down. The blood spots led directly to the gate. Rob stepped into an alley beyond the gate, looking both ways. There was no one to be seen. Evidently Carlos Ramos had gotten away, and it would be a waste of time to try and find him now.

At least Carlos seemed to be alive. How badly he was wounded was another matter. Rob could only hope that he would not be too spooked to call again.

He turned and trudged back to the house. He was sure that it was a waste of time, yet he searched the rest of the house to be sure. He found nothing.

How had the shooter known about the meeting, and

how had he known Carlos would be home? Rob was confident that no one had followed him here; nor had the shooter followed Carlos, either. The shooter had already been here, waiting in the house, before either Rob or Carlos had arrived.

There could only be one answer.

Rob hurried from the house and into his pickup.

*   *   *

A half hour later he had his answer. There was a bug on his desk phone at home. Somebody had been monitoring his calls! That was the reason they knew where he was.

He was filled with outrage at this brutal invasion of his privacy. His first impulse was to rip the listening device out of his phone. But he hesitated. Maybe it would be better just to leave it in place. Now that he knew about it, it might be useful. He just had to be very careful of what he said.

Besides, he wasn't going to be home for the next few days. He knew now what he had to do. He had to go to Mexico, to Juan's hometown, and talk to Juan's wife. Most of all, he needed to talk to Linda Gomez if he could find her.

He sighed. As much as he disliked doing so, he would have to go undercover again. There was no choice. He couldn't go down there as Rob Harding, investigator for the Governor's Task Force on Crime. The likelihood of learning anything in that guise would be nil.

Once again, he would have to be somebody else.

CHAPTER 10

Rob had a number of things to do before he could leave for Mexico. Early the next morning, he called his supervisor from a pay phone, informed him of what had happened last night, and then advised him of what he intended to do.

"I'm afraid that I'll need papers and a new cover. And here I was just getting used to being me again," he said ruefully.

Stanley Morgan asked, "You think that's the way to go, Rob?"

Rob said, "There is no other way that I can see, sir. I badly need to talk to Juan's family, most of all his sister. I have a strong hunch that she knows things that will help our investigation."

"All right, Rob. I'll go along with it. The papers will be ready sometime tomorrow. I'll give you a call, let you know when to pick them up."

Rob said quickly, "Don't call me, sir. I'll call you."

"Why is that, Rob?"

"I've discovered that my phone is tapped," Rob said. "That's why someone seems to always know where I am, what I'm doing."

"Damn! That's going too far!" Morgan said angrily. "I hope you removed the bug?"

"No, I didn't. If I do that, it'll alert whoever is doing the bugging that he's been found out. By leaving the bug in, we may be able to feed him some false information."

"Good thinking. About what happened last night . . . Perhaps I should talk to the Phoenix police and ask them to put out an All Points Bulletin on Carlos Ramos."

"I wouldn't advise it, sir. If we call them and have an APB put out, they'll want to know the whole story," Rob said. "At this point I don't think we should alert them. Carlos isn't wanted for anything except questioning."

Morgan was silent for a few moments, then said, "All right, Rob. We'll do it your way. Call tomorrow about the papers."

A few minutes later Rob was driving to the Ramos residence. There were no signs of life when he drove up before the house, and there was no response to his repeated knocking. The door was locked. There was a narrow walkway between the Ramos dwelling and the house next door. Rob walked down it into the backyard.

The kitchen door that had stood open last night was also locked. Rob peered into the room through the window. He saw no signs of life.

Carlos he hadn't really expected to see, but where was Mrs. Ramos?

He looked down at the ground. He could still make out the blood drops that had to have come from Carlos.

He followed them to the gate. The alley was dirt, and traffic on it since last night had erased any blood droppings that might have shown which way Carlos went as he ran up the alley; not that it made any difference, one way or the other.

Rob turned back into the yard, disappointed. He had badly wanted to talk to Mrs. Ramos . . .

A voice said sharply, "Who are you, señor, and what are you doing in Isabella's backyard?" The voice spoke in Spanish.

Rob turned toward the sound of the voice. Standing in the yard of the house next door was a Latino man. He was old, at least seventy, as thin and wrinkled as a prune. But his dark eyes were still sharp, bright as a bird's.

Rob started toward him, walking slowly so as not to appear threatening. In Spanish he said, "My name is Rob Harding. I'm an investigator for the Governor's Task Force on Crime." He dug out one of his cards and held it out.

The old man took the card and squinted at it suspiciously before looking into Rob's eyes. With a frown he said, "What does Isabella have to do with any crime? She is a faithful churchgoer, gentle as a dove."

"Oh, Mrs. Ramos isn't a suspect in any crime," Rob said hastily. "I wanted to ask her about Carlos. He isn't a suspect, either, but a possible witness." A small but necessary lie under the circumstances. "I knocked on the door, but Mrs. Ramos apparently isn't home."

"No, Señor Harding, Isabella went away last night."

"Went away? Where did she go?"

The man shrugged narrow shoulders. "She did not tell me, and I did not ask."

"Did you see her leave?"

The man nodded. "*Sí*. About nine o'clock last night I

was sitting here in my yard. I get tired of the TV; there is only one Spanish station, and they show things I do not like. I was here when Carlos came home with Isabella . . ."

Rob said quickly, "Carlos brought her home? But his car was sitting in the driveway last night . . ." He broke off as the man's expression became suspicious, and he nodded. "Yes, I was here last night. We'll get back to that in a minute. How did Carlos and his mother come home?"

"In a taxicab, señor. They were in the house not many minutes when they came rushing out. Carlos was carrying one suitcase. They did not speak to me, but I heard them arguing through the open kitchen door. Isabella did not want to leave her home, but Carlos was firm. He said she might be in danger staying here."

"About Carlos . . ." Rob took a breath. "Did he seem all right? Was he wounded or anything?"

"Wounded, señor?" The old eyes became keen. "Why should Carlos be wounded?"

"When I was here last night there was a gunshot from inside the house. I investigated and found a trail of blood leading to the alley. I know Carlos was here at the time. I was supposed to meet with him. Did you hear a gunshot, sir?"

"What time did the gunshot happen, señor?"

"Shortly before eight," Rob said. "I was in my pickup outside. I ran in and found Carlos gone."

"I did not hear the shot. I was watching the TV at that time, and there was a police show on. Cars racing, guns going off, big explosions. It was later when I came outside."

Rob said, "Then I gather from what you're saying that you didn't notice that Carlos was wounded?"

The man shook his head. "I did not see such as that,

señor. Carlos appeared fine."

I know he was wounded, Rob thought, *but apparently it isn't anything serious.*

He said, "Sir, you didn't give me your name."

"My name is Pedro, Pedro Lopez."

Rob nodded. "You have my card with my name and telephone number on it. If you see Carlos or his mother, I would appreciate it very much if you would tell them to call me. It's very important that I speak with Carlos."

Pedro Lopez looked at the card, then said gravely, "I will tell them, señor. I make you my promise."

"Thank you, Pedro. You may be instrumental in solving a murder."

The man smiled widely. "Like on the police shows on the TV, señor?"

Rob laughed. "Something like that, yes."

With a wave of his hand, he went back to his pickup. A block away from the Ramos house, his cell phone rang. Rob picked it up.

"Hello?"

"Rob? This Mary Sue. I have the rundown on Thad Owens and Jed Hawks that you wanted."

"Great! Wait'll I pull over. I'm in my pickup."

He pulled over to the curb, got out his small notebook and pen. "Shoot, Mary Sue."

"First, Owens. This is a man well respected, not only in Arizona, but also in Washington. He has friends and influence in high places, Rob. He's never run for political office, but the man has clout."

Rob said impatiently, "I got all this from Mr. Morgan."

"Just wanted you to know right off the top, sugar, that this is no man to screw around with. Walk carefully."

Mary Sue drew a breath and continued. "His family tree goes back three generations in Arizona. His great-grandfather came to this area in the middle of the last century. He walked in with nothing but a pack on his back. Twenty years later, he was a wealthy mine owner. His son diversified, going into ranching, et cetera. His son, the current Owens's father, bought the land and planted the grove. Which brings us to the present time . . ."

"About time," Rob said snappishly. "I wasn't much interested in his family tree."

"We're thorough here, sugar," Mary Sue said with a laugh. "If you don't want thoroughness, go elsewhere."

"Okay, Mary Sue, I'm sorry," Rob conceded. "All I can do is plead another bad day. Continue."

"As to the present-day Thad Owens, he's clean as new snow; he hasn't even had so much as a traffic ticket. Rumor has it that he's ruthless in business and politics, but loyal and affectionate to his friends."

"He's not quite as ethical as he seems," Rob said tightly. "I know for a fact that he employs Latinos without green cards to work his grove, and he pays the coyote fees to smuggle them across. Not directly, of course, but the money comes from him."

"Sugar, a majority of citrus growers in the country do that, and nobody seems to think less of them for it."

"He's still breaking the law, Mary Sue."

"Big deal. To continue, like I said, he's loyal to people close to him and expects loyalty in return. There have been rumors that he has dealt harshly with people who have betrayed his trust. He has been married once. His wife, Anne, was killed five years ago . . ."

"Killed?" Rob said alertly. "I knew that she was dead, but I didn't know she was killed. How?"

"According to the police report, she was in an automobile accident," Mary Sue said. "The odd thing about it—at least it seems a little odd to me—was that she was killed in the grove itself. She ran head-on into an orange tree. She was unlucky, it would appear. Her only injury was her neck. It was broken in the crash. She was killed instantly."

"She was driving a vehicle in the grove?" Rob said incredulously. "Why in heaven's name would she do that?"

"Apparently Mrs. Owens had a drinking problem. At the time of her death, her alcohol blood count was out of sight, far beyond being legally intoxicated."

Rob sat silent for a moment in thought. What did the fact that Thad Owens's wife, drunk as a skunk, had been killed in an accident have to do with anything?

"Rob? You still there, sugar?"

"Yeah. Sorry, Mary Sue. Is that it about Owens?"

"That's it. Like I said, he's clean."

"Never been busted for drunk driving, anything to do with alcohol? He's a heavy boozer, that I know."

"Hello? Sugar, I told you. Nothing. Zilch."

"Okay," Rob said with a sigh. "Jed Hawks."

"Ah, yes. An interesting gentleman. Papago, as I suppose you know. Born on the reservation not too far from Sells. No siblings. Both parents are dead for some years now. His father also worked for Thad Owens. When the elder Hawks died, Jed Hawks took his place."

"None of that, interesting as it might be, is much help."

"Wait, sugar. Now the good stuff. Jed Hawks has been in a couple of scrapes, arrested twice for assault and battery. I would guess that Mr. Hawks has a temper. The charges were dropped. I suspect that Mr. Owens had a hand in that. Hawks has also been busted three times for being intoxicated. One of those times for assaulting an officer. For that, he served some time in jail. I guess Mr. Owens's influence wasn't enough that time.

"And two years ago, he was arrested for drunk driving. License suspended for one year. In fact, he just got it back two months ago."

"That's it?" Rob asked.

Mary Sue laughed. "Isn't that enough? Nasty man, sugar."

"No argument there. But I already knew that." Rob had a thought. "Does he happen to own a motorcycle? Can you run a quick check?"

"Hold on, sugar." The line went silent for a few minutes.

Rob held the receiver to his ear, drumming his fingers on his knee impatiently.

Then Mary Sue was back. "Sorry, Rob, no motorcycle; the only vehicle registered in his name is a Ford pickup, this year's model."

Rob said slowly, "Thanks, Mary Sue."

"That's why we're here, sugar, to serve the common good," she said cheerfully. "Be careful out there, Rob. It's a wicked, wicked world."

After disconnecting, Rob sat for several minutes in deep thought. Then he put the pickup in gear and drove north and west out of the Phoenix area.

*   *   *

Less than an hour later he guided the pickup down the road between the orange trees on the Owens property. Most of the trees on his left had been stripped bare of fruit. He slowed as he reached the first row still bearing fruit. He could hear the chatter of voices down the line. Shutting off the motor, he got out.

The scene today could have been the same as

yesterday. Except for one thing—Jed Hawks was missing. The pickers were busy in the trees, chattering away like magpies, and Thad Owens leaned against the bin truck, smoking a cigar.

Owens took the cigar from his mouth and greeted Rob with raised eyebrows. "Hello, lad. Didn't expect to see you again so soon."

Rob said, "I wasn't too far away and thought I'd drop by with a question."

Owens said shrewdly, "A question you'd prefer to ask face-to-face, instead of over the phone?"

"Something like that, yeah," Rob said with a wry smile.

Owens shrugged. "Ask away."

"It's about your wife, sir. You told me . . ."

Owens stiffened, his eyes blazing with anger. "What does the passing of my wife have to do with any of this? That happened years ago, for God's sake!"

"I realize that, and it probably has nothing at all to do with the case, but I have to clear it up. You just told me that she died. You didn't say that she died in a car accident and that she was legally intoxicated at the time. Why not, Mr. Owens?"

"Because I don't like to talk about it," Owens said harshly. "Would you tell people about it if your wife had died because she got drunk and ran head-on into a tree? Especially if it happened right in your own front yard, so to speak?"

"No, I suppose I wouldn't," Rob said slowly. "Do you know why she drove her car into the grove?"

Owens said heavily, "Who knows why a drunk does anything? Actually, she drove into a tree just off the road leading to the house, not in the grove itself."

"Do you know why she was drinking so heavily, Mr. Owens?"

Owens stared off into space for a few moments, puffing on his cigar. "Who knows why people do things? I've always been a heavy drinker. Anne told me that she had never tasted alcohol before she married me. But soon after we married, it became a habit for us to have cocktails before dinner. It was only after she was . . ." Owens choked, falling silent, a stricken look on his face. ". . . after she was gone, that I realized she had been matching me drink for drink all those years. It was then, far too late, that I raged through the house. I found liquor bottles hidden all over. I knew then that I may have been responsible, that I put temptation before her and it seized her by the throat." His eyes blazed. "I'm going to have to live with that for the rest of my life."

Rob felt a tug of sympathy for the man. He started to speak, but Owens held up a hand. "I know what you're going to say, lad. Others have consoled me with the same words. You can't lead anyone into becoming an alcoholic. It's something in them, a weakness. Maybe that's all true, but it's no consolation."

They fell silent then. Owens stared at the pickers, but Rob doubted that he really saw them.

Rob said, "Where is Jed Hawks today?"

Owens glanced around, his eyes unfocused. For a moment he didn't seem to recognize Rob. "Jed? Oh . . . He told me this morning that he wasn't feeling well. Came down with a nasty case of the flu. I told him to take time off until he got to feeling better."

Very convenient, Rob thought, *having an employer who gives you time off whenever you want it.*

Owens was looking again at the pickers. Rob started to tell him good-bye, then changed his mind and walked off.

He doubted that the man even knew he'd left.

After leaving the Owens ranch, Rob drove back toward Phoenix, detouring past the apartment building where Janice Rust lived. Maybe Hawks was there again.

As he pulled the pickup into the parking lot alongside the building, he saw someone emerging from the side door. It was a woman; he recognized Janice Rust. She was in jeans and a T-shirt, and she carried a helmet in her hand. She didn't even look his way but went down the building to a parking slot.

He hadn't noticed before, but there was a motorcycle parked there. Janice Rust strapped on her helmet, straddled the cycle, and the motor roared into life. As she pulled out of the slot and started off the lot, Rob made a mental note of the license number.

He debated briefly about tailing her, but it was more important that he talk to Jed Hawks. At the door to her apartment he rang the bell, then knocked loudly, but there was no answer. He gave the bell another jab. Still no answer.

Back in the pickup again, he picked up his cell phone and soon was talking to Mary Sue. He gave her the license number of the motorcycle.

She was back on the line in two minutes. "Sugar, that cycle is registered to one Janice Rust. And to answer your next question, no traffic tickets, at least not going back three years."

"Thank you, Mary Sue, efficient as always."

Rob punched out and sat for a little with the phone still in his hand, but he had run out of people to call.

With a heavy sigh he started the pickup and drove away.

CHAPTER
11

Two days later, Rob was on board a bus from Mexico City, headed for the city of San Juan Mixtepec, located in the state of Oaxaca. The distance between the two cities was 300 miles, and the road was rough, sometimes unpaved. Rob had boarded the bus in Mexico City at midnight last night.

The ancient, yellow bus was packed with men, women, and children, plus a few chickens and even a couple of mangy dogs. The aisles spilled over not only with people, but with piles of produce. The driver's tape player thundered out fast-paced Mexican music, and the passengers raucously sang along with it.

The bus was *segunda clase*—second class.

The bus seemed to Rob to stop every few miles to pick up and discharge new passengers. At each stop the bus was swarmed by children selling soft drinks and tamales. Rob could have looked for a more comfortable vehicle, but he wanted to arrive at his destination as inconspicuously as possible.

He was dressed a little better than most of the other passengers, yet nothing he was wearing was expensive. He was traveling under the name of Pedro Cruz, and he was masquerading as an insurance investigator for a fictitious insurance company with offices in Mexico City. If anyone took the trouble to investigate, his fake identity would be uncovered, but it would take some time. He hoped to be finished and out of Mixtepec long before that could happen.

His cover story was that Juan Gomez had taken out a life insurance policy for a sum equaling two thousand U. S. dollars some time ago with his wife as the beneficiary. The money was due now that Juan was dead, and Pedro Cruz had been sent down to check if the family really existed. It was a weak story and wouldn't hold up on close scrutiny. His hope was that the prospect of insurance money would lull any suspicions or hostility.

Rob felt bad about his masquerade. It was a cruel thing to do to Juan's wife and family, holding out the hope of money to ease their poverty. Perhaps Thad Owens would pay the Gomez family when Juan's killer was unmasked. For all his faults, Owens was generous and seemed genuinely fond of Juan.

Of course, Rob often felt bad about the things he was forced to do when he went undercover. Almost everything he did was based on deceit and lies. Most of the time, he could console himself with the conviction that it was all for a good cause—catching the bad guys. In this case, Juan Gomez hadn't been the bad guy; neither were the members of his immediate family.

The bus pulled into San Juan Mixtepec shortly before noon. The town was a long way from the border of the

United States, yet every year Juan had made the long trek to the border, by bus, by hitching rides, and, Rob suspected, by foot over much of the distance.

Rob knew that the town's population was around 10,000, but he had learned that during much of the year, nearly half of the population was absent, gone north to the States for work or in search of work.

Rob glanced out the window as the bus entered the outskirts of town and slowed to a crawl. What he saw only served to enforce the fact that many of its people spent a great deal of time in the States. Teenagers walking the streets wore blue jeans, T-shirts, and dirty sneakers. The small, concrete-block houses on each side of the street spouted tall TV antennas.

Before Rob left the bus, he asked directions from the driver on how to find the local telegraph office and then headed that way. He knew that the telegraph office was the best place to gather information.

Rob had been a little dubious about how he would blend in here. The people of the state of Oaxaca were the descendants of native Indians, and its three million people spoke ninety dialects. Fortunately, since Rob had Indian blood, he bore a strong resemblance to many of the people he saw on the street. And though he heard a mixture of dialects, he could understand most of what he heard.

The one-room telegraph office was crowded with women, young and old, all wearing gray serapes. A young man stood behind the counter, shouting names and sums: "Dolores Hernandez, one thousand dollars; Angela Lopez, five thousand dollars."

Money from *El Norte*, Rob knew—from Arizona, California, Texas, Florida, and many other states— remittance money for wives and daughters. Rob waited for a bit until there was a lull—the telegraph machine behind the clerk stopped chattering, and the small room almost emptied—before approaching the clerk.

In Spanish he said, "You're busy this afternoon, señor."

The young man grinned cheerfully. "This is the early afternoon. Tomorrow in the early morning, they come in, many more. Most days, twenty thousand American dollars comes in to be given out to the families of those working in *El Norte*."

"Hard times here, is it?"

"Very difficult. The land here, it has been farmed for hundreds of years and now produces very little. There is some good land out in the countryside, but few have the money to buy it."

"My name is Pedro Cruz. I am from Mexico City." Rob held out his hand.

The young man smiled as he shook it. "I am called Alberto Lopez."

"I am here on business, Alberto," Rob said. "Do you know Juan Gomez?"

Alberto's grin disappeared, and he got a wary look in his eyes. "Juan is dead, shot down as he crossed the border."

"I know," Rob said with a nod. "I am an insurance investigator. I am here to talk to his family."

"Juan had insurance?" Alberto said in surprise. "That hardly ever happens."

Once again, Rob felt a pang of guilt about his deception, but he plunged ahead. "It seems he did. He must have had great love for his family."

"Oh, yes, Juan's family was his whole world."

"The thing is, I don't have his address, so I thought I'd come to the local telegraph office." Rob smiled. "I know that you know much of what goes on."

Rob held his breath as Alberto studied him closely.

Would Alberto wonder why there wasn't a home address for the Gomez family on the insurance policy?

Then Alberto grinned, swelling with pride. "That is true, Señor Cruz. I know everything."

Alberto gave Rob directions on how to find the Gomez abode; Rob thanked him warmly and left the building. Outside, he breathed a sigh of relief. So far, his flimsy story had held up. He had counted on everybody being so pleased about the policy that they wouldn't bother to question the story.

It was only a half-mile walk to his destination. He was surprised to find a large crowd gathered in the front yard before a small adobe building. Children ran about in the yard, and adults sat on the porch. They were mostly women with a few older men. They were drinking soft drinks and beer, and two chickens simmered in a large black kettle suspended over a wood fire. All the adults were dressed in somber clothing; the women all wore black.

Rob introduced himself as Pedro Cruz to one of the old men. Then he waved a hand around. "A celebration, señor?"

The man shook his head mournfully. "No, a farewell. A farewell to Juan Gomez, the man of the family."

"Oh. I should have known." Rob cleared his throat. "Being from the city, I tend to forget such things. Could I have a few words with Señora Gomez?"

The man's faded eyes narrowed in distrust. "Maria is grieving, señor. This is not a time to disturb her with worldly matters."

"I can respect that, but my visit is business that concerns all the family. I have journeyed all the way from Mexico City."

Rob hoped he wouldn't have to explain more because

this man, despite his age, was shrewd and would likely see through his story for the lie that it was.

But after a moment the man turned his head and spoke to a teenage girl lounging in the doorway. "Take this man in to see Maria, Angela."

Angela nodded, motioned for Rob to follow her, and went into the house. Rob followed her into a house cool in dimness and scented with heavy incense. What seemed like a hundred candles burned in the room. Niches in the walls were filled with the figurines of saints, each with its own candle. Women all in black moved about with hushed voices and a faint rustle of clothing.

Angela led Rob down a short hallway and to a half-open door. She rapped on the door and stuck her head in. "Maria, there is an important man from Mexico City with important business to see you."

A broken voice murmured faintly. Angela stood back, and Rob went past her. Again, the room was lit by flickering candles. The room's only occupant was a woman in black kneeling by the bed in an attitude of prayer.

Now she stood up painfully, her face shrouded by a black veil. In a voice hoarse from many tears she said, "This is not a time for business, señor. My husband is dead. It is a time for saying prayers for his soul."

"I know, señora, and I am sorry for my intrusion. But it is about your husband that I have come. I work for an insurance company, and your husband had a policy with our company."

A gasp came from Maria Gomez, and her hand swept the veil up from her face, which had a look of disbelief. "Juan had an insurance policy?" Despite her load of grief, there was a look of great dignity about her.

"Yes," Rob said. "Juan seemed to be a man who wanted

above all else to take care of his family."

"My Juan lived for his family," she said simply. "Every year he went to *El Norte*. Every month while he was away, he sent money. Every year he paid money to buy the ranchito for us."

By this time Rob was seated in the bedroom's one chair, and Maria was perched on the edge of the bed. Now he sat up alertly. "He was buying a ranchito?"

Maria said proudly, "It is a small plot in the hills above town. It has good soil. He wanted to grow corn and beans and melons. What we could not eat, he would sell in town. During his time at home, he had been building a house for us. It is almost finished. Then he would have been with us the year round."

Rob asked, "He had intended to quit his job with Señor Owens?"

Again she nodded. "*Sí*. This was to have been his last year going to *El Norte*. He had promised me."

"Did anyone up there know of his intention to quit?"

"No, señor. He was afraid that they might try to stop him."

"Stop him?" Rob frowned. "Why would they want to do that?"

Maria looked away, staring at the small window opening onto the back. The laughter of children at play came through the window.

Maria glanced back at Rob, her face shadowed with sorrow. "I have not yet told the *niños* about their papa's death."

Rob could think of nothing in reply to that. Instead he said, "Why would someone want to stop Juan, Maria?"

Maria shook her head. "I do not know. Juan did not say. He was strange when he returned home last year."

"Strange? In what way?"

"He . . ." The woman hesitated, searching for words. "Juan usually was full of stories about his time away from us. He told me everything that happened. This time, he said nothing. For six months, he said nothing. When I tried to ask him, he got angry. Juan never got angry at me."

Rob felt a stab of disappointment. He had expected that Juan would have confided in his wife, would have told her something that would have pointed to his killer.

He said, "Señora Gomez, you know that Juan was murdered?"

"*Si.*" Her breath caught, and she looked away. Rob saw a tear trickle down her cheek. "Linda, Juan's sister, told me. Señor Owens called her."

"Did Juan ever tell you anything about someone wanting to kill him?"

Maria shook her head violently. "No, no! Who would want to kill Juan? Everybody liked him!"

Rob wanted to make the standard response to that remark, "Somebody didn't," but he refrained. He realized that he had struck out here; and if he asked any more, Maria Gomez was going to start to wonder why an insurance man was asking such questions.

He said, "Maria, there was no telephone number for your home on the insurance policy. There was a number for Juan's sister, Linda. I called that number, but it was disconnected. Since I couldn't talk to either of you on the phone, I came here. Is Linda Gomez present here today?"

Maria shook her head. "No, she did not come. I sent one of the *niños* to tell her about the farewell to Juan, but she was not at home."

"You have any idea were she might be?"

"No, señor, I do not. I am worried about her. She and Juan were all that is left of their family, and Linda is heavy with grief and rage."

"Rage? Why is she angry?"

Maria Gomez had already begun to retreat from him, returning to the core of grief inside her. She gave a weary, distracted shrug. "I do not know."

Rob got to his feet. "I will disturb you no further, Maria. Once again, I am sorry for your trouble."

As he left the room, Rob was certain that the woman slumped on the bed was unaware of his departure. For her, the rest of the world no longer existed.

On the porch Rob said farewell to the people there and offered his condolences for the death of Juan Gomez.

Fortunately, Rob had gotten an address for Linda Gomez from Mary Sue before leaving Phoenix; she had gotten it through her contact at Telmex.

The address was a two-story apartment building located about a mile from the Gomez house. The apartment was on the second floor. Rob had toyed with the thought of asking Maria Gomez for a key but had discarded the thought at once. Why would an insurance investigator want admittance to Linda's apartment?

One of the first things Rob had taught himself after going to work with the task force was ways to get through a locked door. It was not legal, of course, even in the States. Here, in another country not too friendly to Anglos, it was a serious risk. If he got caught, he could be locked into a jail cell, and the key thrown away.

Rob had to know about Linda Gomez. It was a mystery as to why she had disappeared after learning of her brother's death, and Rob had the feeling that Linda might have the clue he badly needed.

The apartment building was neat and well cared for. Flowers bloomed in a colorful riot all along the front. It was the middle of the afternoon now, the time of the well-known afternoon siesta. The apartments were all quiet, shuttered against the drowsy afternoon heat.

Rob encountered no one on the stairs going up to the second floor, and the hallway outside Linda's apartment was empty. There wasn't a sound coming from any apartment. To be on the safe side, he knocked on the door and waited. No sound of stirring inside.

He went to work on the lock. It wasn't complicated, and he had it open in less than a minute. He let himself into the department and locked the door after him.

The living room's blinds were closed tightly, and the room was dim and cool. From somewhere in the back he heard a grandfather clock ticking, and then a rather noisy refrigerator kicked on.

The room was furnished rather cheaply, all in light colors. The rugs on the floor were bright, woven. Bright prints of Mexican scenes hung on the walls. There was a small TV set like a blind eye against one wall.

It was a cheerful room, and Rob knew that it would be even more cheerful with the blinds open, flooding it with sunlight. Clearly, Linda Gomez was a person not much given to gloom. One thing did strike him—unlike the homes of many Latino people, there was no religious art to be seen. No religious scenes in the prints, no niches set with religious statues, lit with candles.

He moved down the small hallway toward the back. There was a kitchen with a table and chairs. No dining room. A bathroom was beyond the kitchen, and there were two closed doors on each side of the hall.

He opened the door on his left first. It was clearly Linda Gomez's bedroom. There was a regular-sized bed with a colorful spread and a cross on the wall above the headboard. At least Linda wasn't a nonbeliever.

A chest of drawers was against one wall. He only opened a couple of drawers. They were packed with the usual, and the closet next to the chest was filled with clothes. There was even a suitcase on one shelf.

Rob stood for a moment in thought. It would appear that she hadn't left for good; she would have taken more clothes. He didn't really know what he expected to find here, but whatever it was clearly wasn't in this room.

He went across the hall to the last room. This one seemed more promising. There were filled bookcases against two walls and a couch that could be made into a bed. But most promising of all was the desk in one corner, holding a small computer.

His eyes were caught by a picture on the wall above the computer. He took it off the wall, clicked on the light over the desk, and studied it closely. The picture was of two people, male and female, posed before a house. Rob was almost positive that the house was the one he had left not too long ago.

The pair had their arms around each other, smiling into the camera. Written in small letters in one corner were the words: "Juan and me—Christmas 1990."

Linda Gomez looked to be around eighteen in the picture; Juan was at least ten years older. Linda had a heart-shaped face with long hair black as ink and dark eyes that held a promise as old as time itself. Rob sensed a happy nature, a bright sense of fun, and a sharp intelligence. She was someone that he felt sure he would like to meet.

Juan's face was narrower, and even then his hair was beginning to thin. Although their coloring was much the same, Juan was darker. The result of all those years of laboring under the fierce Arizona sun, Rob thought. And despite his smile for the camera, it struck Rob that there was a solemnity behind the smile, as though he carried responsibilities beyond his years.

Rob sat down at the computer and clicked it on. It didn't take him long to discover that it served mostly as a word processor.

He punched up her file list. His pulse rate quickened at one listing, titled simply "Juan."

The document was less than a page. Most of it was a summary of Juan's years spent working for Thad Owens, including the address and phone number of the grove owner.

What followed was a series of one-liners; after each was a question mark.

"What happened last year that was so traumatic to Juan?

- Thad Owens?
- Jed Hawkes?
- Hoby Macklin?
- Sonoyta?
- Lukeville?"

Rob leaned back, staring at the list of names followed by question marks.

He knew now where Linda Gomez had gone, and he was also reasonably sure that he knew what she intended to do. She was putting herself in grave danger.

CHAPTER 12

It took Rob two days and nights to make it from San Juan Mixtepec to Sonoyta by a combination of air travel and bus. It was an arduous journey, made even worse by his worry that Linda Gomez had already made her way across the border into the United States.

There was one factor in his favor: he was fairly certain that Hoby Macklin wasn't making as many smuggling trips as was his custom. Hoby Macklin—or Tobe Marvin—had to know that he was wanted by several law enforcement agencies and would be lying low. Yet Macklin had to have income to survive, and Rob had learned that most criminals on the run stick to their usual criminal endeavors when they need money.

Rob was still Pedro Cruz, but he was no longer posing as an insurance investigator. He had torn up and discarded all of the false identification and carried no identification whatsoever. He was now a "wetback"

126

named Pedro Cruz, and he was looking for a coyote to smuggle him across the border.

Rob had also discarded the clothing he had worn as an insurance investigator, and now he wore faded jeans, a short-sleeved shirt, none too clean, a worn denim jacket, and heavy, worn work shoes. Although he doubted there was much danger of being recognized, he wore a floppy straw hat tilted low over his face, and he had not shaved for two days.

Sonoyta, directly across the border from Lukeville, Arizona, was a honky-tonk town. The main street was lined with dusty, odorous saloons, small liquor stores catering to Americans coming across to buy tax-free liquor, and shops full of crucifixes and strong-smelling garlic.

Rob had no trouble blending in. The street thronged with Latinos waiting for transport across the border. There were even some women and small children. Rob looked at every female face, seeking to match it with the picture of Linda Gomez he had seen in her apartment.

Arriving in Sonoyta in early afternoon, he wandered the main street until dark seeking Linda with no success. He lingered on the edges of a group of men congregated to discuss their hopes of jobs in the States, the coyotes to contact, and the ones to avoid. There was no mention of Hoby Macklin.

There was every possibility, of course, that if the man was still operating as a coyote, he had assumed a new name. *If that's the case*, Rob thought, *I'm out of luck.*

Late that afternoon, tired and hungry, he ate a so-so meal in a small cafe, but it was filling and took the edge off his weariness. The cafe also had three pay telephones on the back wall. Rob waited until none of the three phones was in use and punched out the number for Research at the task force.

When the call was finally put through, and the phone was answered, he said, "Mary Sue? This is Rob."

"Rob! How are you, sugar?" she said. "More important, where are you? I haven't heard from you in . . . What? Four days?"

"I'm still in Mexico," he said glumly. Briefly, he sketched in what had happened, what little he had learned. Then he said, "Did you finish the check on Tobe Marvin?"

"Yes, but I found little to help you. Tobe Marvin is a native of Phoenix, born and raised. No record, no black marks. After high school he worked various jobs. Auto salesman, auto mechanic, service station attendant. He even managed to make manager of a chain gas station. He was let go after two years, reasons unknown." She laughed. "Not very successful, Mr. Marvin. That happened about ten years ago. Then he dropped right off the earth. Not a word about him since."

"That was probably when he began switching identities," Rob said. "Any prints on record anywhere?"

"Not that I can find. I did finally get a report back from the FBI on the fingerprints for Hoby Macklin."

Rob said, "But since we have no prints for Tobe Marvin to run a match, it doesn't do us much good."

"That about says it, sugar," Mary Lou said, "except for one thing: we got a report that a black van was found yesterday, abandoned in Mesa. It had been reported stolen the day before Juan Gomez was murdered."

"The license plates, were they stolen as well?"

"You got it."

"And it was wiped?"

"Clean as the proverbial whistle."

Rob sighed. "Can't say I'm surprised. That van was hot enough to start a forest fire."

"How long you going to be south of the border?"

"I don't know. Not long, I hope."

"You want me to connect you with Mr. Morgan, Rob?"

Rob hesitated, looking around. One of the other two phones was now in use. Rob lowered his voice. "No, I'll talk to him later. You can fill him in on what I told you. And thanks, as always, Mary Sue. Don't know what I'd do without you."

Her laugh was soft and warm. "That's what all the men say."

*   *   *

When darkness fell, men began to drift off the streets and toward the river bottom just outside of town. There weren't that many rooms to be rented in town, and Rob knew that most of the men couldn't spare what money they had for lodging. Since it was summer, the nights were quite warm, so sleeping outside was no hardship.

On the way Rob passed through the outskirts of the town. It was a landscape of shacks made of tin and cratewood. After the shacks came empty spaces of barren dirt and gravel. Chickens scratched in the dirt, and he could smell burning charcoal.

Rob strolled down to the river bottom. It was full dark now, and a number of cooking fires flickered like fireflies in the night. Rob estimated that at least fifty men, women, and children were sitting around the fires. The odors of beans and stew meat cooking hovered around the fires, mixed in with coffee brewing.

Since Rob had already eaten, he didn't try to join any of the groups huddled around the fires. He idled about from fire to fire as inconspicuously as possible. Without making a point of it, he tried to check out the faces of the women against the image of the picture he had seen of Linda Gomez. Every one of the women wore men's clothing; they either had their hair bound up in bandannas or hidden by hats pulled low.

Rob could understand why they wanted to hide behind male attire; women alone crossing the border placed themselves at high risk. It was not unusual to see reports in the media about Latino women being sexually abused, raped, or even killed while attempting to cross the border.

It would be easy enough, Rob knew, for Linda Gomez to disguise herself. She could have dyed her hair, put on a pair of glasses. She could even be wearing colored contact lenses if she wanted to go that far. It would be especially easy to hide here at night around the campfires.

Besides, he had no way of knowing that she was here. She could already be across the border, or he could have misread the situation entirely; she might not try crossing the border at all.

Discouraged, Rob was about to search for a place to bed down for the night. He was standing a few feet away from one fire when a voice spoke to him in Spanish: "You look lonely out there by yourself, amigo. Want to join us for a cup of coffee? It is not the best, but it is hot and tastes like coffee, anyway."

Rob was happy to make contact with one of the migrant workers, but he hesitated long enough to show reluctance. Then he strolled over and squatted by the fire. There were only four men around the fire. Two of them were passing a bottle back and forth and were clearly on the way to becoming drunk. The fourth one was nodding off.

The one who had called to Rob said, "I'm Manuel. These guys . . ." He waved a hand around. "I do not know their names. The two sharing the bottle are interested in the liquor, whatever it is, and the other man hasn't introduced himself either."

"I'm Pedro Cruz," Rob said, accepting a tin cup of steaming coffee.

Manuel held up a cautioning hand. "Around here, Pedro, first names are the safest, next to a name not your own." Manuel laughed softly. "Who knows when one of us may be in the pay of the Border Patrol or Immigration."

Rob frowned. "I have never heard of them doing that, Manuel."

Manuel laughed again. "Neither have I, my friend, but anything is possible. All the gringos have to do is put a bounty on our heads, and we will have Border Patrol men sneaking across to tag us even before we cross."

Rob laughed with him. "Oh, I don't think it will come to that."

Manuel drank coffee. "Do not be too sure, my friend."

"How many times have you crossed, Manuel?"

"How many? Let me see . . ." Manuel closed his eyes in thought. It was difficult to guess his age, but Rob estimated that Manuel was a few years past fifty.

Manuel opened his eyes and said, "This time will be twenty-three, Pedro."

Rob whistled through his teeth. "You're a veteran at this, aren't you?" He took a sip of coffee before saying casually, "Do you always use the same coyote?"

Manuel gave him a sharp glance. "Never. That way they get to know you."

"But I always thought that it was better that way. Find one you can trust and use him every year."

"You cannot trust any of them," Manuel said sharply. "Not only gringos, but those of our own kind. A Mexican coyote who lives in the States will dump you into the desert to die as quickly as would an American." He looked at Rob. "How many years have you done this, my friend?"

"This is my first time."

Manuel nodded. "So I thought. You have much to learn."

They were silent for a few moments, drinking coffee. Rob noticed that it had grown late. Most of the fires had died down, and people were sleeping. Some were rolled up in blankets, and Rob even saw a couple of sleeping bags, but the majority were sleeping just on the ground. He could understand that. Even if they had the money for blankets or sleeping bags, it would be unwise to bring with them anything that couldn't be carried on their person. Theft was common, even among their own.

After a bit Rob said casually, "Manuel, have you ever heard of a coyote by the name of Hoby Macklin?"

"That one!" Manuel spat into the dying fire. "He is a bad one, my friend. Stay away from him. Just a week ago he left men in the desert to die. He even shot one."

Rob looked at him closely. "Do you know that for a fact?"

Manuel gave a shrug. "I was not there. I have never used that one to get me into the States, but I have heard the stories. Everyone knows of Hoby Macklin."

"Well," Rob said, "perhaps he is already in jail for murder."

"He is not in jail, and he will be smuggling some of these men across tomorrow night."

"Do you know that for . . ." Rob changed directions. "But how can they trust such a man if they know what he has done?"

"Because they are desperate," Manuel said simply. "There are never enough coyotes to go around. Some of these men . . ." Manuel waved a hand around. "Some of them have been waiting for days."

After a moment Rob asked, "I am ashamed I am so stupid, but I do not know how to even approach a coyote."

"There is a man in town who will put you in touch with a coyote," Manuel said. "He is always at a cantina, called Tequila Sunrise, before the noon hour. He will handle it, but you must have the money to show him and to pay his fee. You will need at least a thousand dollars, American money."

"Does he also act for this Hoby Macklin?"

Manuel shook his head. "Yes, but do not use that one, my friend. Not if you value your life!"

Rob knew that it would be a mistake to pursue it further. After a moment he said, "Maybe it would be best to make it across on my own. Just walk across the border . . ."

Manuel was shaking his head again. "That would be a big mistake, Pedro, even more so for a beginner like you. You might make it across all right, although not that easy. The border is patrolled closely for those who walk across. But they cannot stop every truck that crosses and search it. They do not have the manpower.

"But let us say you do get across and avoid the Border Patrol. Where would you go from there? It is a long walk across the desert to where work can be found; that is why so many of us die. The coyotes at least deliver you to the places we work or to where we can find work."

*   *   *

The first thing Rob did early the next morning when he went into town was to call the task force. This time he talked directly to Stanley Morgan.

"I need a thousand dollars wired immediately to the

telegraph office here in Sonoyta, sir. I hope to contact Hoby Macklin and cross the border with him."

"The money will be on its way when I hang up, Rob," Morgan said. "But I'm not sure I approve of what you're about to do. I know that I give my investigators room to operate on their own, but I do wish you had discussed this with me first. I agree with you that it is necessary to find this sister of Juan's, but this business is dangerous."

"I've traced Linda Gomez, sir. Now I think that she will be crossing the border with Macklin. This way if I can arrange to be smuggled in with them, I can make contact with both."

"I'm surprised that this Macklin is back in business. He must know that we're looking for him."

"He's probably desperate for money, sir," Rob said. "His kind always stick with what they know. He may be hoping to pick up enough money to get out of the country."

Morgan sighed. "Rob, if Macklin is that desperate, you're going to be placing yourself in great danger."

"He has to be questioned, sir, as well as Linda Gomez," Rob said.

"But isn't he likely to recognize you, Rob?"

"It's doubtful. If he's seen me, it's been at a distance, and I'm wearing the clothes of a grove worker."

"Okay, Rob. If you think that's the way to go."

"I do, sir. At the moment it's the only move I have."

*   *   *

The Tequila Sunrise held only a half-dozen customers when Rob walked in shortly before noon. The place was dark, smelling of spilled beer, cheap liquor, and cigarette smoke. Rob had just come from the telegraph office and had a thousand dollars folded in his pocket.

The man he wanted to see was easy to find. He sat in a booth in the back, an aging man, at least fifty pounds overweight, with dead eyes and a face that looked greasy in the dim light. His hair was going, and what few strands were left were combed over the bald spot like dark strings.

Two men, clearly Latinos looking for transport across the border, were in the booth with him, and Rob had to wait ten minutes before they finished their business and left. Just before they left, Rob saw a wad of bills slipped into the fat man's hand.

Rob took the seat vacated. The fat man looked at him with dead eyes.

Rob leaned close and spoke in a soft voice. "I need to get across the border. My cousin in Phoenix, he wrote he had gotten a job for me with his patron."

"Your cousin, why didn't he make arrangements with his coyote?" the fat man asked.

"He has no use for coyotes," Rob replied. "He has a green card. He lives there."

The fat man was silent for a few moments. "It will take much money. A thousand dollars."

"I have the money," Rob said. "But my cousin, he said that I should ask the name of the coyote, so he would know who to expect. He said I should ask for one named Hoby Macklin."

The fat man was silent again. Then he nodded. "All right, the coyote who will take you across tonight shall be Hoby Macklin."

Rob felt a leap of triumph; at the same time he was surprised that the man would still be using the name of Macklin. Yet Rob had learned that criminals often were arrogant in their belief that no one could touch them;

they believed themselves invulnerable to police, holding firm to their view that no policeman was smart enough to catch them.

Rob said, "It will be tonight then?"

"Yeah." The fat man held his hand across the table, rubbing thumb and forefinger together. "If you have the dough."

Without a word Rob took the ten hundred-dollar bills from his pocket and placed them in the fat man's hand. He knew that he would never see the money again and felt a fleeting regret. This man did all his dealing with illegals on this side of the border and would never cross into the United States where he could be arrested and the money confiscated.

The man was speaking again. "Just a mile outside of town on the main road is an abandoned service station. Be there at eight sharp tonight. Hoby Macklin will pick you up there. He will be driving a van. Be sure and be there on time. He will not wait for you. If you miss him, don't come to me for your money back."

Getting to his feet, Rob said, "I will be there, señor. It is important that I get across the border."

*   *   *

Rob arrived at the abandoned gas station at a quarter to eight. He was carrying a cardboard suitcase packed with old newspapers. There were no personal things in the suitcase; he knew that any illegal going across the border would likely be carrying at least some personal belongings, and a cardboard suitcase was normal. His straw hat was pulled down low, and he wore sunglasses, which again wasn't unusual, even after dark.

Rob didn't know how effective his attempts at disguise would be, but there was always the chance that Macklin knew him well enough to recognize him. After all, somebody driving a black van had been following him around Phoenix.

The van arrived precisely at eight, but it was gray, not black. Evidently, Macklin had decided to change colors. The van was clearly new, as it was wearing temporary license plates. Rob had to marvel anew at how stupid some criminals could be.

He didn't rush out at once but lingered back in the shadows. After a moment he was glad he did. A car drove up behind the van, a pink Cadillac several years old. Two people got out of the vehicle. One, the driver, was the fat man Rob had struck the bargain with in the saloon. The other was slight, slender, with a scarf wound around the head, and wearing a small backpack.

The fat man had switched off the lights of his car, and Rob couldn't see enough of the figure wearing the scarf to decide if it was male or female. He emerged from the shadows of the ruined building and headed for the van. The fat man had opened the back doors, and the figure wearing the backpack had clambered in.

The fat man turned at the sound of Rob's footsteps. "Ah, there you are," he said in a low voice. "Just in time."

He gestured, and Rob climbed into the van. Just as the fat man started to close the door, the figure of a man came around from the front of the vehicle. The fat man closed the back door before Rob got a good look at the van driver.

Rob could see the figure of the other passenger huddled near the partition between the driver's seat and the rest of the van. Instead of moving to the front Rob placed his ear against the back door. He could hear enough to make out the words spoken.

An angry voice that had to belong to Hoby Macklin

said, "Two passengers? That hardly pays enough to make the trip!"

"I am sorry, Señor Macklin," the fat man said in a whining voice. "But that is the best I could do. You gave me very little notice . . ."

"Did you use my new name?" the snarling voice demanded.

"What name is that, señor?"

"You didn't, did you? Damn it, you used Hoby Macklin! That name is poison down here after what happened last week. You stupid idiot, next time I'll use another go-between!"

The fat man whined, "I forgot the name you told me . . ."

"Never mind," Macklin snapped. "I'll make new arrangements next time."

Rob heard hard footsteps going down the side of the van. The door opened and slammed closed. The motor caught, and the van screeched away, gravel rattling against the undercarriage.

CHAPTER
13

The van was traveling very fast. There was no way to see outside for the back windows had been painted black. The only light coming in was from a small window opening into the driver's compartment. Rob could see the small figure of the second passenger huddled against the front wall only dimly.

His earlier guess had been correct; the van was new. It had the smell that only new vehicles have. Rob had the strong suspicion that the vehicle had been stolen. That only increased the risk that they might be stopped by the State Highway police. It was more than possible that the plates had been stolen from another vehicle.

He realized that this meant that Hoby Macklin was truly desperate. He had risked everything on a roll of the dice. He had hoped for a full load of illegals so that he could collect enough money to finance his flight from Arizona, perhaps even out of the country.

This thought caused Rob to realize something else: there was a strong possibility that Macklin considered his two passengers expendable. Why risk getting caught with them? He already had their money. Some time within the next hour, it was entirely possible that he would pull off into the desert and murder Rob and the other passenger.

Was Macklin ruthless enough to do that? The answer was yes. He had killed already; what difference would two more make?

Rob made his way to the front of the van on his hands and knees; once he lost his balance and rolled against the side of the vehicle as it took a sharp corner at high speed.

He leaned back against the side of the van beside the figure. The backpack had been removed. He said in English, "The way this guy drives, we may not make it in one piece."

"No habla English," said a voice muffled by the scarf.

"Oh, I think you do," he said. Switching to Spanish, he added, "You're Linda Gomez, Juan's sister, aren't you?"

A gasp escaped from behind the scarf, and the woman moved away a few inches. Rob scooted after her.

Keeping his voice low, he continued in Spanish, "Señorita, we're after the same thing here. I want to learn who murdered your brother, and I'm sure you do as well."

The scarf was lowered, and dark eyes peered at him. This time she spoke in English. "Who are you?" Her English was perfect, without an accent.

"My name is Rob Harding. I was just down to San Juan Mixtepec, looking for you. I talked to Juan's wife, Maria. When I learned that you had left suddenly, I followed you here."

Her voice gathered strength. "How did you know I'd come here?"

Rob laughed softly. "You made a mistake, Miss Gomez. You left a list of questions on your computer, a list of names. One of those names was Hoby Macklin, the man driving this van. I had a hunch that you'd come here, looking for him."

"You broke into my apartment?" she said, outraged. "What gave you the right to do that?"

"Legally, I had no right, but in the interest of justice, I figured I had no choice. And you should look at it the same way. Don't you want the murderer of your brother caught?"

"I still don't know why you're interested. Are you a cop?"

"In a way, yes. I'm an investigator for a recently formed Governor's Task Force on Crime . . ." He went on to tell her briefly how he had become involved.

She was silent for a moment. "What led you to me?"

"Lola, Thad Owens's housekeeper, told me that your brother seemed upset, at least different, when she talked to him just before he was killed. She thinks that something happened last year when he was in the States. Even his wife, Maria, told me that he seemed distant. She said he usually told her everything that happened while he was working in the States. This time, he told her hardly anything. I thought I should talk to you. Did Juan tell you about anything unusual that happened?"

Her voice hardened. "What if he did? Why should I tell you?"

He took her arm in a firm grip. "Because it may have some bearing on his killer. So far, I haven't been able to come up with any motive at all for his murder."

Linda Gomez shook her head stubbornly; the scarf fell away from her face. In that moment the van passed under a streetlight, and he could see her clearly for just a moment. Her features were delicate, yet there was strength and a keen intelligence reflected there. Her eyes were dark pools.

For a moment Rob was distracted by her beauty. She was a very lovely woman, and despite the strange circumstances, Rob felt a strong pull of attraction.

He gave his head a sharp shake. This was hardly the time for such thoughts.

"Linda, talk to me!" He gave her arm a sharp shake. "Did Juan tell you anything at all about something unusual happening to him?"

"Whatever my brother said to me is between us."

"He must have told you something about Hoby Macklin, because that's why you came so far to see him. Isn't it?"

She remained silent.

Rob leaned close, his mouth next to her ear. "Linda, listen to me. Even if Macklin doesn't know you're Linda Gomez or that I'm an investigator looking for him, the odds are good that he may drive off-road anytime and kill both of us. Or leave us to die in the desert."

"Why would he do that?" she said in a whisper.

"Because he's a desperate man. Because he badly needs money. He came down expecting to take back a full load of illegals. Instead, he has only two. Plus he has our money. The chances are good that he won't even bother delivering us; why not just eliminate us? Hoby Macklin is a ruthless man, Linda."

Linda was quiet for a moment. Then she sat up, trying to peer out the small window in the rear of the cab. She slid back down and whispered, "Are we in the United States now?"

"Oh, yes, we passed across the border long ago," he said. "We're in the middle of Organ Pipe now."

In the faint light he could see a frown of thought on her delicate features. Then she sat up and pounded on the partition.

He took her arm and pulled her away. "What the hell are you doing?" he said in a fierce whisper.

She jerked out of his grip and again knocked on the partition.

The van slowed, and the partition slid open. In a harsh voice Macklin said, "What do you want?"

"I have to go," she said in heavily accented English. "The bathroom. It is . . . painful!"

"Too bad," Macklin said with a chuckle. "No bathrooms along here, *chica.*"

"Then I will have to do it in your vehicle," she said.

Macklin muttered a curse, and the van slowed even more.

"What are you doing, Linda?" Rob said in a growling voice. "What are you thinking?"

Linda said, "I know what I'm doing."

The van came to a jolting stop, and angry footsteps sounded down the side of the vehicle. Then the back door was flung open. Hoby Macklin scowled in at them.

"You'll have to use the bushes, lady," he said. "Seems to me you should have known you were in for a long trip and made allowances . . ."

Linda Gomez had already scrambled across the van to the back door with astonishing agility, dragging the backpack with her. Macklin had to step back to let her out. Rob saw her hand dip into the backpack.

"Hey! You are in a hurry, ain't you?" he said with a laugh.

He broke off with a grunt, taking another step back. "What the devil are you . . . ?"

Rob had made it to the back now, and there was enough light to reveal what was happening. Linda had a knife out, the point against Macklin's belly.

"I want to know what happened to my brother, and you're going to tell me!"

Her hand moved slightly, and Macklin winced. "Hey! Careful with that thing, lady!"

"Then talk to me. Tell me about Juan."

"Juan? Juan Gomez? I had nothing to do with that."

For the last few seconds Rob had been aware of headlights coming up fast from behind them. He had scrambled out of the van now and stood right behind Linda. The sound of the fast-approaching vehicle rose to a roar.

Linda said tensely, "You're lying. The story is, you killed him!"

"The story has it wrong, lady," Macklin held up his hands in entreaty. "I swear . . ."

Rob spoke in English, "Why don't you just tell us what happened that night, Mr. Macklin?"

Macklin stared at him with astonishment. "You're not a wetback! What's going on here?"

The approaching vehicle rounded a curve fifty yards back, bathing them in bright light. Slowing, its tires spun on the side of the road. It came to a stop ten yards back, and a spotlight came on.

Macklin reacted with alarm, shrinking back against the van. Belatedly, Rob realized what was happening. He seized Linda by the arm and jerked her out of the spotlight beam. Macklin remained frozen in the light as a gun roared twice. The bullets struck him, throwing him back against the van. Blood spouted from his chest as he slid slowly to the ground.

The spotlight beam left him, probing the shrubbery beside the road. Rob had already pulled Linda into the darkness.

She resisted, pulling back. "What are you doing, Harding?" She had opened the backpack and now stored the knife in it.

"Don't you see what is happening? Macklin has just been killed, and we're next. Keep going," Rob urged.

He had never carried a gun on any of his task force investigations; now he wished that he had one. The only weapon they had was the knife Linda had, and that would be of no use against the gun carried by the driver of the vehicle with the spotlight.

Linda, as if finally realizing the danger they were in, began to run, plunging into underbrush. Rob hurried after her. The roar of the vehicle rose to a crescendo, and the spotlight probed the night behind them.

Rob realized with a chill that the vehicle was following them into the desert, or at least trying to follow. Rob pressed his hands against Linda's back, urging her on.

They ran into the night. Something loomed up before them, a frightening monster with long arms, rising to an incredible height. Linda came to a stop with a faint scream. Rob collided with her, then put his arms around her from behind before he realized what stood in their path.

"It's a saguaro," he said in a hoarse whisper. "Let's keep on. They're trying to follow in their vehicle."

"They?" she said. "Who's they? What's happening here?"

He guided her around the saguaro. "I believe it's the person, or persons, who shot your brother, Linda. I think we're wrong about Hoby Macklin. Oh, he may have been involved in a minor way. Certainly he knew what really happened. It's clear that he was the primary target here tonight. They wanted to eliminate him."

"Then why are they trying to track us down?" she asked as they hurried on.

"The obvious answer is that we were witnesses. They don't seem to like witnesses."

She said, "But we don't really know anything. At least I don't. All I saw was a car with a spotlight, and I saw Macklin killed. But I don't have any idea as to who the killer is."

"Neither do I, but he's clearly not one to take chances." He took her hand and drew her to a halt. "Let's listen for a moment."

They stood looking back the way they had come. It was a dark night; a small sliver of a moon was hidden behind a thin cloud cover. Rob could no longer hear the sound of the racing motor, and there was no glow of light. Apparently their pursuer had turned off the headlights. Had he given up the chase?

Then Rob heard the sound of dry underbrush cracking and the faint sound of cursing. Apparently their pursuer had blundered into some dead desert underbrush.

"He hasn't given up yet," Rob muttered. "Let's move on, but move quietly."

"Where? Which direction?" Linda asked.

Rob nodded to the east. "That way. Into the desert. For now, anyway. If we try to circle back to the highway, we may stumble onto one of them. We don't know how many there are."

They set out again at a rapid pace but slow enough to avoid stumbling into the desert plants. It wasn't long before they were truly in the desert. Organ pipe and saguaro cacti loomed around them like alien visitors springing up out of the desert.

Rob didn't know what time it was, but it had to be well after midnight. Once again, he wished that he had a weapon so that he could make a stand somewhere and fight back.

He thought it ironic that they should be running into the desert, just like the illegals who had died out here several days ago. Had the person who had shot Juan chased after the others? Or had he been satisfied with killing Juan and not really interested in the other illegals? Had the killer assumed that they would die in the desert, which was what had happened?

Somehow, Rob felt that Juan Gomez had been the main target, perhaps the only target. He had felt that from the beginning, and he had learned nothing since that had changed his mind.

They had been running steadily for some time and were well out into the desert; they hadn't heard any sounds of pursuit behind them.

Rob reached out and caught Linda's arm. With heaving breath he said, "Let's catch a break."

They stood for a few moments, listening. They could hear nothing but the sounds of the desert at night: the eerie hoot of an owl, the slithering sound of some desert creature underneath their feet, the beat of the wings of a nightbird overhead, and in the distance, the lonely wail of a coyote.

The moon broke through the clouds momentarily, and Rob spotted some boulders a few yards away. He motioned with his head. "Let's sit on those for a bit. Poisonous reptiles are supposed to be diurnal, but let's not take any chances. At least on the rock we can draw our feet up out of the sand."

"Anything to get some rest," Linda said with a sigh. "But aren't we taking a chance they might catch up to us?"

"I think they've broken off the chase. Anyway, I'll keep alert. If I hear anything, we're off and running again."

Linda removed the scarf and shook her hair out. It was black and long, a jet fall down her back. Points of light from the moon glinted off it.

After a few minutes of silence had passed, Rob asked in a low voice, "You speak very good English, better than many born in the States; how did that come about?"

"I learned it, how else?" she said tartly. Then she relaxed a bit. "I attended the University of Mexico, and English was my second language. I wanted to become a teacher and teach the children English." Her voice took on a harsh note. "Since half or more of our people go to the States to work every year, it seemed to me that knowing how to communicate with the gringos would be valuable."

"That makes sense," Rob said with a nod. "And did you? Become a teacher, I mean?"

"Yes, I've been teaching for four years now."

"In San Juan Mixtepec?"

"Of course. It's my home. I was born and raised there," she said.

"And your brother . . . Did you teach him English?"

"Oh, yes, it wasn't hard," she said, smiling. "Juan was already good in English from all his years working in Arizona. He would have been somebody if my family could have sent him to school. But they could not."

"But you managed to attend school," Rob commented,

"all the way through college."

"That was through Juan. He helped as much as he could without depriving his family. He was a hard worker and good at managing money."

"When he came back from the States last year, he was changed." Rob leaned toward her. "Maria told me."

Linda hesitated for a few moments. "Yes, he was."

"In what way?"

"Things had changed in America, Juan said."

"Generally, or for him?"

Linda made a startled sound. "Why, for him, of course. He didn't confide in me as much as he usually did. He said that he would tell me everything when he was sure."

"Sure about what?" Rob demanded.

"I don't know!" Linda pounded her fist on her knee in frustration. "He wouldn't tell me. He just said that he had learned something that might make working for Thad Owens impossible, but he wasn't yet sure. He said that was really the only reason he was returning this year, to find out the truth. But . . ." Her voice went flat. "Now he never will, will he?"

The sound of grief in her voice tugged at Rob. He reached over and took her hand. "Maybe now, together, we can find out the truth, Linda."

"But it will be too late for Juan," she said drearily.

"I know. Linda . . ." He waited until she looked up at him. "Juan must have told you something about Hoby Macklin, or you wouldn't have come looking for him. Lola, Thad Owens's housekeeper, told me that Juan was unhappy with him and was thinking of using a new coyote. Was that true?"

She nodded. "Yes. Juan said that he didn't trust him any longer."

"But why?"

"I don't really know," she said. "The only thing he said was that this Macklin could be connected with the other thing troubling him."

"And yet he used him for the last trip. Why is that?"

"He told me that it would be the last time, that if he continued to work for Owens, he would find another coyote." She added in a hard voice, "I know it's not all that easy to find a dependable man to smuggle people across."

Rob felt his frustration mount. "It's all so damned mysterious! If your brother was feeling these misgivings, why didn't he act on them? He might still be alive."

"The only thing I can tell you is that Juan was fiercely loyal, loyal to people he worked with, people he had known for years." Her voice turned bitter. "I told him more than once that he might come to regret trusting gringos!"

They fell silent for some time. After a bit Rob looked at his wristwatch. It was closing on two o'clock.

Linda said abruptly, "How long are we going to stay here?"

"I figured we'd wait until daylight, just to be on the safe side, and the rising sun will orient us. Then we'll make our way back to the highway and flag down a car. When we get to a phone, I know a Border Patrol guy . . ."

Linda stirred in protest. "Not the Border Patrol! They'll send me back across."

"No, they won't." He squeezed her hand reassuringly. "I'll tell the guy you're working the case with me. It'll be okay, I promise." He laughed suddenly.

She glared at him. "What's so funny?"

"I was remembering you threatening Macklin with that pocket knife. What did you think? That you could scare him into confessing?"

"It might have worked, given a chance," she said defiantly.

"You have sand, Linda, I'll give you that." In a sudden gust of anger he struck his thigh with his fist. "Damn it, there's one thing I can't understand about this. How did the shooter back there know we were coming across tonight with Macklin? Unless, of course, the target was Macklin and had nothing to do with us."

After a few moments had passed, he glanced at her, struck by her sudden silence. "Linda?"

She sighed softly. "I told Jed Hawks when I talked to him several days ago."

Rob reared back. "You told Hawks? About seeking out Hoby Macklin?"

"Yes," she said with a nod. "Maybe I shouldn't have, but I had just learned about Juan, and I was upset, nearly out of my mind with grief."

CHAPTER 14

Clint Barker responded to Rob's call and picked them up at the rest stop, not too far from where the shooting had taken place. Barker had already been informed of the murder of Hoby Macklin and was on his way to the crime scene when Rob had reached him on Barker's car phone.

The van and Macklin's body had been discovered at dawn by a passing truck driver. By the time Barker, Rob, and Linda arrived on the scene, the body had been removed and the van towed away. Only the crime scene technicians were there, scouring the area for clues.

After thirty minutes on the scene, Barker realized that he wasn't needed there, and he drove Rob and Linda to Tucson where Rob could rent a car to drive to Phoenix.

On the drive, Barker listened without interruption as Rob told him what had happened. Rob omitted one fact—Linda's telling Jed Hawks of her plan to arrange with Macklin to smuggle her across the border.

When they parked before the car rental place, Barker looked first at Linda and then at Rob.

"If I did my duty here, Rob," Barker said, "I'd drop you off and turn right around and drive Miss Gomez back across the border."

"No!" Linda cried. "Rob, you promised . . ."

Rob held up a staying hand, without looking at her. "Come on, Clint. You have a certain discretion in these matters. It isn't as if Linda had committed a crime."

Barker said sharply, "It's a crime, Harding, to sneak across the border without the proper permission."

"Clint . . ." Rob drew a deep breath. "Give her a little space. Her brother was murdered, and last night she saw another man shot down before her eyes. If nothing else, have some compassion."

"Don't try to con me, my friend," Barker said. "I feel for her very much, or I would have driven south of the border first before driving you up here. But you'll have to admit, Miss Gomez, that what you did was foolish. You're lucky you weren't killed."

"Foolish maybe," Rob said, "but understandable."

"And you were foolish too, Harding," Barker added. He sighed. "Okay, she stays, but you're responsible for her."

Rob nodded. "I told you I would be. Aside from everything else, I need her; Linda may hold the key to this case."

Barker looked at him keenly. "In what way? Have you told me everything?"

"Everything that's important," Rob said quickly.

"Seems to me you're no closer to solving this thing. Your undercover gig down in Mexico was a waste of time," Barker said with a short laugh. "The only result is that we have another dead body, Hoby Macklin's."

"Macklin would have been killed eventually. And we know something important we didn't know before. We know now that Macklin wasn't our killer."

Barker frowned. "You don't know that for sure. He could have had a partner."

"It's possible," Rob conceded. "But I doubt it. I think the same person who killed Juan Gomez also killed Macklin last night."

"You have a candidate for that?"

Rob shook his head. "Not for sure, only a possible."

"Another feeling, Harding?" Barker said dryly. He glanced at his watch. "But never mind. Just be sure to keep me informed."

"I will, my word on it."

Rob and Linda got out of the car, and Barker drove off as they went into the building to arrange for a car to take them to Phoenix.

*   *   *

It was late afternoon when they arrived in Phoenix. Linda dozed most of the trip with conversation kept at a minimum. She roused when they entered the outskirts of Phoenix and looked about with interest.

"Is this your first time in Phoenix?" Rob asked.

"It's my first time in the States at all," she replied. "Juan told me several times that, with my education, I could probably get a green card and qualify for a teaching certificate here if I tried, but I wasn't interested." She glanced over at him. "You didn't tell the man from the Border Patrol everything. You didn't tell him that I told Jed Hawks that I was contacting the coyote, Macklin, to smuggle me in. Why didn't you do that? Because you didn't want to reveal how foolish I was?"

"I could lie and say yes, just to be gallant." He grinned over at her. "But my concern was not to save you embarrassment. I didn't tell him because I now think that Hawks is our killer, and it's my case."

"I'm glad you didn't tell him," she said with an expulsion of breath. "I came into your country to avenge my brother; I intend to kill this Jed Hawks myself!"

"Hey, whoa now! Let's don't be so bloodthirsty, Linda. I can appreciate how you feel. But even if we find out for sure that Hawks killed Juan, you would be breaking the law if you killed him."

"I don't care!" she said harshly.

"Besides . . ." He laughed aloud. "How would you kill him, Linda—with your trusty knife?"

She glared at him. "Are you mocking me?"

"No, not at all." Still smiling, he added, "Well, maybe a little. Actually, I was hoping to lighten things up a bit."

"I'm in no mood to lighten up, Mr. Harding!" she snapped. Then she began to smile, the first time he'd seen a smile on her face. "That did sound pompous, didn't it? I'm sorry, Rob." She placed a hand lightly on his arm. "I've been in a black mood since hearing of Juan's death. Maybe it's time I was letting up a bit. I certainly shouldn't take it out on you. I'm beginning to realize how much I owe you. I would probably have been dead but for you. I felt like a deer frozen in a spotlight back there last night, and on my own I would probably have stood like that until I was shot down too."

"Listen, I was scared too. But I've been in such situations before, and I know when fast reactions are required."

Linda said, "And I appreciate the effort you're taking to find Juan's murderer."

"It's my job," he said simply.

He spotted the logo of the rental car place up the block and slowed down to make the turn into the lot.

Linda sat up in alarm. "What are you doing?"

"I'm turning the rental in. We don't need it now; I have transportation of my own at home."

"But I thought we were going to the Owens ranch to confront Jed Hawks!"

"We will do that, Linda," he said mildly. "But not today."

"Why not?"

"Because it's late afternoon. By the time I go home, get my pickup, and drive up there, it'll be well after dark."

She stared at him. "And so?"

He parked the car and shut off the motor. "Linda, neither one of us is in very good shape. I've gone over twenty-four hours without sleep and so have you, except for those catnaps you've taken on the drive up."

"I'm fine," she said stoutly. "I can keep going."

"Perhaps I could too, but neither one of us would be very alert. Besides, I have some phone calls to make. We're taking a cab to my place, where we'll clean up. Then we'll go out and have a relaxing dinner, after which we'll get a good night's sleep. We'll tackle Jed Hawks in the morning. He's not going anywhere."

"I'm not staying in your house!" she said hotly.

"It's not a house, Linda, it's an apartment. It only has one bedroom, but there's a pull-out in the living room; I'll sleep there. The bedroom has a lock, which should keep you safe should I turn into a raving beast, which I very much doubt, the way I feel. Okay?"

Linda's skin had darkened, and she was looking away

in embarrassment. She mumbled, "Okay."

"Fine. Now I'm going to check the car in. I see that they have a lounge. You go in there. Relax. Have a cold drink while I use the pay phone."

"Don't you have a phone at home? Can't you wait until then?"

He smiled tightly. "My home phone is tapped."

Her mouth fell open. "Tapped! But you're a policeman, why don't you . . . ?"

Rob was already getting out of the car and didn't answer her. Inside the office he pointed a finger at the small lounge, and Linda went into it with a resigned shrug. Rob finished his business at the desk, then went to a pay phone in a corner of the lounge.

Once again, he bypassed speaking to Stanley Morgan and asked for Research. "Hi, Mary Sue."

"Rob! Sugar, where are you? We've been going crazy here. Mr. Morgan is mad enough to chew nails."

"Because I decided to get myself smuggled across the border without checking with him first?"

"However did you guess?" she said dryly.

"I guess you'd better switch me over to his office," he said with a sigh.

"Won't do you much good," she said airily. "He isn't in today."

Rob stared at the phone. This was unheard of. Stanley Morgan spent almost every waking hour in his office. He said, "Mr. Morgan is always there, you know that."

"He went on a brief vacation this morning."

"And he never takes a vacation."

"That's the reason he's taking this one. He hasn't taken a vacation since he put together the task force, and that's been over two years. His wife put her foot down. She told him that if he didn't take a couple of weeks off and take his family somewhere completely out of touch, she'd scream all the way to the sanitarium."

"Mr. Morgan told you that?" he asked incredulously.

"No, she did. But he did give me a phone number and told me to contact him if you needed him badly enough. Do you, sugar?"

"No, no," he said hastily. "I'll just fill you in. First off, I don't suppose you've got the word yet. Hoby Macklin is no more. He was killed last night."

Briefly, he brought her up to date on all that had happened since he'd talked to her last.

"My, you have been a busy little bee, haven't you, Rob? So what's next on the agenda? Jed Hawks? Am I right that you think he's our killer?"

"It's beginning to look that way. Of course, I've been suspicious of him all along, but I still can't pin down a motive for him to kill Juan Gomez," Rob said. "Last night's killing of Hoby Macklin I can understand. Clearly, he knew too much."

"Anything else you want me to tell the boss?"

Rob made a startled sound. "But you just told me he was away, out of touch with the office!"

"Officially, yes, and also as far as his wife is concerned." Mary Sue laughed softly. "But he'll slip away and call in. He's fastened to this office on a long leash. In fact, I'm surprised he hasn't called in yet today."

"Just tell him I'm making progress," Rob said. "Hopefully, I'll have the case wrapped up by the time he returns to work."

"Will do, sugar. And you be careful out there, you hear?"

Rob hung up the phone and faced around. He saw

that Linda Gomez was giving him a look that could only be described as baleful. It was after five. For a moment he toyed with the idea of giving in to her impatience and driving out to the Owens ranch to grill Jed Hawks.

He shook his head sharply. He was hungry and tired and badly in need of a shower. It would be much better to tackle the job in the morning, well-rested.

He strode across the lounge to her. "Ready to go, Linda?"

"Ready to go where?" she snapped.

"Linda . . ." He heaved a sigh. "We've already gone over that. We're going to have dinner. Then we're going to have a good night's rest. In the morning we track down Jed Hawks. What is it that you don't understand?"

"I understand all of it," she said sullenly.

"Good! Now I'm calling a taxi, and we're getting out of here."

He turned on his heel and returned to the pay phone. He looked up the number for the nearest cab company and punched it out.

He looked back over his shoulder at Linda as he waited for a response. She was sitting upright, staring straight ahead, a scowl on her face. He was beginning to like Linda—perhaps too much—but she could be aggravating. Very aggravating!

*   *   *

Two hours later they were seated in a restaurant a mile from Rob's apartment, where they had taken showers and changed into clean clothing. Linda had simply changed into another pair of slacks and a blouse, a little better than the rough work clothes she had worn before, but not much. At least her hair was loose and flowing past her shoulders, no longer bound up in the scarf, and she had added lipstick and a touch of makeup.

She looked very attractive, Rob thought, and yet he had to wonder how she would look in a dress. Had she even brought a dress along in her backpack? Probably not. He didn't dare ask. Besides, he reflected wryly, she might consider it a sexist question.

Despite her statement that she wasn't hungry, he noticed with amusement that she ate heartily. They had both ordered steaks and all the trimmings. They ate mostly in silence, which Rob thought was just as well if Linda was still as hostile as she had been since he'd told her they weren't going after Jed Hawks until the morning.

Finally Linda leaned back with a sigh. "That was very good, Rob, thank you; I didn't realize I was so hungry."

"The last time you ate was down in Sonoyta, right?" he asked.

She nodded. "That's right."

"And you didn't think you were hungry?"

"I had other things on my mind." There was a return of the earlier tension to her voice and manner.

"Relax, Linda," he said, smiling. "Relax and enjoy yourself a little while you're here. You might even come to like *El Norte*."

"I doubt I'll be here long enough," she said. "I'm an illegal, don't forget."

"Oh, I haven't forgotten. But after this thing is over, I'll report to my supervisor, Mr. Morgan, how much help you were to solving the case, and he may be of some assistance toward your getting a green card."

"Maybe I don't want to become a green-card citizen," she said tartly. "Did you ever consider that?"

He shrugged. "That, of course, is up to you. But there is one thing you should think about."

She peered at him suspiciously. "And what might that be?"

"There are a great many children, Latino children, in this country who need the kind of help you can give them. Especially here in Arizona."

Linda slumped wearily back in her seat, yet her dark eyes still snapped with fire. "Right now, all I want to think about is catching the man who killed my brother."

Rob nodded. "I'm with you on that." He caught the eye of their waitress and made a scribbling motion in the air. "First, we need a good night's rest. So let's get out of here, okay?"

*   *   *

Back in the apartment Rob got Linda settled in the one bedroom. "Lock the door, so you'll be safe," he said dryly.

"It wouldn't matter," she snapped. "I'm perfectly capable of protecting myself."

"Oh, I know that, Miss Gomez. I've seen you in action, remember?"

She closed the door in his face without answering. He waited for a moment, listening for the click of the lock. When it didn't come, he laughed softly to himself, got sheets and a pillow out of the linen closet, and carried everything into the living room. He opened the pull-out couch and made a bed.

Although tired, he lay awake for quite some time, his thoughts on Linda. He was more and more attracted to her as time passed, yet he knew that no relationship would ever happen between them. Once the matter of Juan's killer was settled, she was on her way back to Mexico.

With that thought, he drifted into a deep sleep untroubled by dreams.

Some sound wakened him some time later. He sat up, glancing at the luminous dial of his watch on the coffee table. It was almost one o'clock.

What had aroused him?

He listened intently but could hear nothing. He got up, put on his robe, and padded down the hall. At the door to the bedroom, he put his ear to the panel. Nothing.

He knocked and called softly, "Linda?"

There was no response. A premonition seized him, and he threw the door open, feeling along the wall for the light switch. In the flood of light he saw that the bed was empty. Her backpack was gone as well.

He swore aloud. There was no doubt in his mind as to where she had gone—in search of Jed Hawks.

He could understand her burning desire for revenge, yet it was a stupid thing to do. She was placing herself in grave danger; Hawks wouldn't hesitate to kill her.

Another thought struck him, and he hurried into the living room and to the chair where he had draped his pants. He felt in a pocket and experienced a rush of relief as he felt the keys to the pickup.

Linda must have walked to the nearest pay phone and called a cab. Rob was dressed and out of the apartment within ten minutes, diving into his pickup. He reached into the glove compartment, got the slap light, and clamped it on the top of the cab.

He started the pickup and roared up the street, the light flashing red in the night.

CHAPTER
15

The traffic was very light, and Rob was able to travel fast. The few vehicles on the streets pulled over at the sight of the flashing light. He considered calling the local police and sending them to Owens's residence; they could reach there before he could. In the end he decided against it.

If the police came and found an illegal on the Owens property, they would call in Immigration, and Linda would be shipped back to Mexico immediately.

It took him less than a half hour to reach the Owens citrus ranch. He swung onto the lane leading to the house dangerously fast. Even late as it was, lights blazed in the main house. His intention had been to drive to the small house where Hawks lived, but he changed his mind and skidded to a stop before the main house.

Thad Owens must have heard the pickup, for he opened the door before Rob could ring the bell. Even this late he was fully dressed in faded jeans, a sports shirt, and cowboy boots. There was a glass of dark liquid in his hand. He must have still been up when Linda knocked on his door.

"Well, lad," Owens said with raised eyebrows. "Why am I not surprised to see you?"

"Has Linda Gomez been here, Mr. Owens?"

Owens nodded. "Just left about five minutes ago. She was in a taxi. You didn't see it leaving?"

Rob shook his head. "What did she tell you?"

"She demanded to see Jed Hawks. I told her he wasn't on the place tonight."

"Did you tell her where she might find him?"

"Yes, I did, lad. I was a little reluctant. She had a wild look about her, but she's just a little bit of a woman." Owens chuckled. "I figured that Jed could handle her. And she told me she wouldn't leave until I told her where Jed was." He sobered. "Woman told me she was Juan's sister. That true, lad?"

Rob nodded without speaking.

"She's come up to root out his killer, hasn't she? Not satisfied with the progress you and the other cops are making? You have anything to do with her getting across?"

Rob smiled tightly, remembering. "You might say that I had something to do with it, yes."

"But why is she looking for Jed? What connection did he have with Juan's death?"

Something tickled Rob's mind. He was silent for a moment, trying to pull it out, but it wouldn't come.

"Lad?"

Rob said, "You'll have to ask Hawks that. Where is he?"

"I'm not sure. I haven't seen Jed in a couple of days. I just know that he isn't back there in his little house."

"Where did you send Linda?" Rob demanded.

"The only place that I could think of where he might be," Owens said. "His girlfriend's place. Janice Rust."

Rob hesitated, staring at Owens searchingly. Something was slightly off here, but he couldn't put his finger on it.

He said abruptly, "Thanks, Mr. Owens." He turned and hurried down the steps.

"Wait, Harding!" Owens called. "What's this all about? What's going on here?"

Rob hurried on without answering. He'd left the motor of the pickup running; he got in now, made a quick U-turn, and sped down the lane between the rows of orange trees. All those he could see were bare of the fruit now, and he concluded that the orange picking was finished.

As he covered the short distance to where Hawks's girlfriend lived at a fast clip, Rob worried over his decision about not calling for assistance. The one thing Stanley Morgan had drilled into the minds of his investigators was to call for backup whenever venturing into a potentially dangerous situation.

Was this a dangerous situation for Linda?

He didn't think so, yet he could be wrong. The fact was that she was being foolhardy by rushing headlong into a confrontation with Jed Hawks and could be said to deserve whatever happened to her. But that didn't matter. If she were harmed in any way, Rob knew that he would always blame himself.

By the time he had thought all this over, he was in sight of the apartment building where Janice Rust lived. Pulling into a parking slot near the entrance, Rob worried about his indecision. He had never hesitated about making a decision, and he never agonized about it afterward when it turned out to be wrong. Stanley Morgan commented to him once: "I like that trait in you, Rob. I wish all my investigators had it. In this business you must make instant decisions, right or wrong. Too much hesitation and you may lose either a suspect or your own life!"

Then Rob realized why he found making a decision in this instance so difficult; this was the first time that he cared enough about somebody to be this concerned about them. Did that mean he was falling in love with Linda Gomez?

If he was, he was making a big mistake. The moment this was over, Linda would be back in Mexico like a shot! She certainly wasn't about to become involved with a gringo who lived in the States, even if he could be considered only half gringo.

He shut off the motor, got out, and hurried toward the entrance to the building. As he approached the door to Janice Rust's apartment, he saw that the door was open, light streamed out of the apartment, and he could hear loud, angry voices.

He stepped into the doorway. In the middle of the room Linda was confronting Jed Hawks. Hawks was wearing a robe, his hands jammed into the pockets. Janice Rust, wearing only pajamas, stood to one side, watching with a stunned expression.

"I know you killed my brother!" Linda screamed in Hawks's face.

"Lady, you're crazy, mad as a hatter . . ." Hawks broke off as he saw Rob in the doorway. With a sardonic grin he said, "Hey, bro! Why don't you come in and join in the fun? And close the door—Janice doesn't need her neighbors hearing all the nasty accusations this lady is making."

Rob took a few steps inside. With a hand behind his back, he groped for the door handle and closed the door, but he did not close it entirely. This was a potentially explosive situation, and he might want to leave suddenly with Linda in tow. A second lost unlocking the door might prove fatal.

"Well, now, isn't this cozy?" Hawks said. "Oh, I forgot to introduce the crazy lady, Linda Gomez. But then you know her, don't you, Investigator Harding?"

"How do you know that, Hawks?" Rob asked. "The only way you could know that was if you were the gunman who shot Hoby Macklin down in Organ Pipe. Isn't that right, bro?"

Hawks scowled at him. "What are you talking about? You're sounding as crazy as she is!"

"I'm not crazy!" Linda shouted. She moved closer, right in his face. "You killed my brother!"

"Lady, you have my sympathy, and I can understand you being upset," Hawks said. "But I didn't kill Juan. What earthly reason would I have to kill him?"

Rob stepped up and took Linda by the elbow, holding her back. He said, "That bothered me too. Now I think I've figured it out. From what Juan told Lola Mendoza, his wife, and Linda, he saw something, heard something, or learned something that disturbed him deeply. I believe it had to do with you, and you killed him to keep him quiet. You killed Macklin last night because he knew that you'd murdered Juan."

"Bro, you should be writing movie scripts," Hawks said with a sneer. "What an imagination!"

Rob had been watching Janice Rust out of the corner of his eye. She was growing increasingly agitated. He spoke directly to her. "Miss Rust, was Hawks with you last night?"

"Of course I was!" Hawks said. "Tell him, babe."

Janice backed up, her hands held up. "Don't involve me in all this!"

"You won't be involved if you tell the truth, Miss Rust," Rob said. "But if you lie, you will be. Did he spend the night with you? And did he borrow your motorcycle several nights ago—Tuesday, I believe?"

"Why, yes, he did borrow my cycle."

She was interrupted by Hawks: "Janice! Babe, you don't have to talk to this guy! He's not even a real cop."

"I'm real enough to pin these murders on you, Hawks."

Hawks wasn't listening. He had locked stares with Janice Rust in a silent battle of wills.

Rob spoke softly into Linda's ear, "When you arrived at Owens's house, was he in bed? Did he answer the door in pajamas?"

She stared at him curiously. "Why, yes. I got him out of bed. He came to the door wearing a robe. Why do you ask?"

"I'll explain later." He raised his voice. "Miss Rust, you have to realize your position here. If you lie and give Hawks an alibi, you could be charged with aiding and abetting a murderer."

"Don't listen to him, babe!" Hawks said forcibly. "He can't do anything. He's got nothing!"

Rob recalled something an old-time cop had told him once: The weakest link a suspect has is with the one he loves, be it male or female. If push comes to shove, they usually cave.

"Miss Rust, Jed Hawks is at least twice a killer," Rob said quietly. "If he wasn't with you last Tuesday night, he was down in Organ Pipe shooting a man to death. Do you want to lie for a man who'd do that?"

Janice Rust backed another step, her eyes wild with growing panic. "It wasn't supposed to happen like this, Jed! I came to accept Mrs. Owens's death, but you swore to me that it wouldn't happen again!"

Rob said quickly, "Mrs. Owens, Miss Rust? What happened to her? Her death wasn't an accident?"

"Janice!" Hawks warned in a harsh voice.

But Janice Rust was in full flood now. "Jed tampered with her car—the brakes or steering, I don't know—but whatever it was caused her to lose control and ram into the tree!"

"Damn it, Janice, I told you to shut up!" Hawks snapped. His hand came out of his robe pocket holding a .38 revolver, the same type of gun that had killed Juan and Macklin. Hawks said, "Now I'm going to have to . . ."

Her voice became shrill with hysteria. "If you hadn't got drunk and blabbed so that Mexican worker could hear you . . ."

"Shut up, Janice!" Hawks raised the gun. "One more word and I'll have to kill you; I don't want to do that."

"Put the gun down, Jed," said a voice from behind Rob. "Just put it down now."

"I thought it was about time you were showing up," Rob said, turning slowly.

Thad Owens stood in the doorway, a weapon of his own in his hand. Rob recognized it as a Colt .45, enormous and deadly. Owens, never once taking his gaze off Hawks, came on into the room, closing the door behind him.

Hawks had swung around and stood gaping at Owens, his gun pointing at the floor. Then he visibly gave himself a shake and said sarcastically, "What if I don't? You going to shoot me?"

"If I have to." There was a faint tremor in Owens's voice.

Hawks's gaze swung to Rob. "See what happens when you work for the white man, bro? Don't do what he says and he threatens to shoot you."

"Jed," Owens said wearily, "just put the gun down."

Instead, Hawks began to raise the gun until the muzzle was centered on the grove owner's chest. Without warning Owens fired. The bullet struck Hawks in the right shoulder and threw him back against the wall. The gun flew out of his hand, and he slid down the wall to the floor, staring numbly at the blood seeping through his shirt.

"This has all gone on long enough," Owens said dully.

Rob said, "You going to kill all of us, Mr. Owens?"

Owens blinked at him dazedly. "What?"

"Something's been bothering me for some time," Rob said. "I know now that Hawks killed those people, but I could never figure out the motive. Now I know; he did it at your orders. First, your wife had become an embarrassment and a liability, so you had him fix her car so she'd be killed. Juan inadvertently found out, so you ordered Hawks to kill him. And Hoby Macklin knew Hawks had shot Juan that night, so last night Macklin had to die. You said something several days ago that finally clued me in.

"You said, 'For I sure as hell want you to catch that van-driving scum who murdered poor Juan.' How did you know the killer drove a van? You knew because Hawks stole a van for the job, drove the van when he tried to kill me, then dumped it. Tonight the final nail was driven. When you were rousted out of bed by Linda, you were in robe and slippers. Yet when I came by shortly after she left, you were fully dressed. You were about to follow her over here."

Linda made a sound. "You! You had Juan killed?"

She took a step toward Owens, and Rob took her arm, restraining her. "Take it easy, Linda." To Owens he said, "Why did you have Hawks rig your wife's car?"

Owens had been staring at Hawks, and now he glanced at Rob with a start, as if he hadn't heard a word Rob had said. "What? Annie?" His eyes began to burn. "Annie was a drunk, a disgrace to the Owens name! Besides, she was having an affair. Drunk and unfaithful. She was making me a joke among my friends. They were laughing at me behind my back. I had to put a stop to it!"

"There's always a divorce," Rob pointed out.

"If I had filed for a divorce, that would have only made it worse, airing our dirty linen in public," Owens said with a grimace. "She threatened to raise a stink if I tried to divorce her. No, it was the only way."

"But the act bound you and Hawks together, didn't it? He could blackmail you, take time off from work, whatever."

"Yes, damn him!" Owens glared at Hawks, lifting the .45, which had been pointing at the floor. Hawks, as though sensing the renewed threat, glanced up and cringed in fear.

Rob said, "You know, of course, that you're as much legally responsible for the last two deaths as he is?"

"Yes, I realize that." Owens's finger tightened on the trigger. "I should kill him. I should kill all of you!" He glared in turn at everyone in the room.

"No, Mr. Owens," Rob said gently. "You're not a killer. I saw your reaction after you shot Hawks. You can only order it done; you can't do it yourself. You don't have it in you to kill us. Here, give me the gun."

He took a step toward the man, his hand held out. He

stared directly into Owens's eyes. The eyes were glaring, defiant, and then the defiance leaked out, leaving the eyes vacant and unfocused. The hand holding the gun sagged, and Rob took the gun away. He led Owens, now completely docile, to the couch. Owens sat, face in his hands; his shoulders shook in silent sobs.

Rob glanced around and spotted a telephone on a table against one wall. He took Linda by the hand and led her across the room with him.

"Linda, do know just how foolish you were?" he said in a low voice. "You could have been killed, charging out here alone!"

Her dark eyes blazed at him. "I don't care! I . . ." Then her shoulders slumped, her anger draining away. "You're right, I was stupid. But since Juan was killed, it's been like I've had a raging fever. Now . . ." Her glance went to Owens on the couch, to Hawks slumped against the wall, semiconscious. "They're going to pay, aren't they?"

"Yes, Linda. Both of them." He squeezed her hands. "Now stay right here. Don't wander off again. I have to make some phone calls."

First he called 911, asked for an ambulance to be sent to Janice's address, and reported a shooting.

Next, he called Mary Sue's number at the task force. Since it was long after midnight, he got her answering machine. "Mary Sue, this is Rob Harding. The case is finished. I've uncovered the killers, and the local police are on their way to arrest them. Would you contact Mr. Morgan and let him know? I'll give him a full report when he gets back."

*   *   *

It was four days after the scene with Jed Hawks and Thad Owens. On learning what had happened, Stanley Morgan had rushed back to Phoenix. Rob had spent three of those days tracking down Carlos Ramos. When he had found him, Carlos said he had overheard a drunken Hawks confessing his responsiblity for the death of Mrs. Owens. Carlos was more than willing to testify to that fact.

When Rob reported to his boss, Stanley Morgan said sternly, "Rob, you acted unwisely, charging in without backup; you know my orders on that."

"Yes, I know. But I thought it best under the circumstances." He hid a grin. "It worked, didn't it?"

"Are you being impudent, young man?" Morgan scowled for a moment, then relaxed. "Of course you're right; it worked out okay. But you've done this before, Rob. Someday you're going to get burned, barging into situations like that on your own."

Rob asked, "What's happening now with the case?"

"Oh, we have them cold," Morgan said with a shrug. "The Rust woman is talking; we can't shut her up. Hawks is willing to talk if he can strike a deal to avoid the death sentence." He laughed. "That .38 he had, the dim brain used it to kill both Juan and Macklin!

"Thad . . . well, he isn't saying much of anything. He seems to be almost in a coma. But we've got him in a box, damn him!" Morgan struck his desk with his fist. "Who would ever have figured that a man I'd called a friend since childhood could do these things?"

"How about Linda Gomez?" Rob asked. "I haven't seen her since it happened."

"She told us all she knows. She said she was going back to Mexico, but that she would come back to testify if she was needed . . ." A knock sounded on the door. "Come in!"

The door opened, and Linda Gomez came in. Rob got to his feet in surprise. "Linda! What are you doing here?"

Her face flushed dark at the sight of him. "I didn't know you'd be here, Rob. I came to speak to Mr. Morgan."

Morgan also got to his feet. "Not that I'm not happy to see you, Ms. Gomez, but I thought you'd gone back to Mexico."

"I changed my mind," she said softly, her gaze on Rob.

Rob felt a leap of happiness. "You're staying here?"

"You said you thought it would be a good idea."

"I think it's a great idea," Rob said, feeling a foolish smile spread across his face.

"And you also said that perhaps Mr. Morgan would help me toward getting my green card?"

Morgan said heartily, "I'd be happy to do what I can."

Linda had advanced into the room to stand before Rob. In a voice barely audible she said, "Is it what you wish, Rob?"

"It's what I wish very much."

They fell silent, staring deep into each other's eyes.

After a few moments Morgan cleared his throat. "I have a suggestion. Why don't you guys go somewhere and have lunch, and I'll make a few phone calls in Linda's behalf?"

"Okay with you, Linda?" Rob asked.

"It's more than okay with me, Rob."

He took her hand, and they went through the door without once looking away from each other.